THE HOLIDAY Claus

ANN EINERSON

Paperback ISBN: 978-1-960325-10-5

Cover Design by @madicantstopreading
Dev Edited by Jeannine Colette, @probablyalovestory, @bookswithkaity, @bryannareads
Edited by Rebecca @Fairest Reviews Editing Services, Tina Otero, Lyndsey Goss, @thecozy.homebody
Proofread by Courtney DeLollis
Formatted by Champagne Book Design

To the hopeless romantics who believe in the magic of love, especially under the mistletoe, I hope you enjoy this swoony holiday love story with Brooks and Lila!

PLAYLIST

I'll Be Home—Meghan Trainor
Underneath the Tree—Kelly Clarkson
Candy Cane Lane—Sia
Winter Things—Ariana Grande
white xmas—Sabrina Carpenter
Sleigh Ride—Ella Fitzgerald
Mistletoe—Rosie Darling
Santa Tell Me—Ariana Grande
It's Beginning to Look a Lot Like Christmas—Alexander
Thoma

AUTHOR'S NOTE

Hey, Reader!

Thank you for picking up *The Holiday Claus.* The holiday season has always been my favorite time of year, so naturally I had to write another sweet and spicy novella because nothing pairs better with mistletoe and snow than a dash of romance and holiday cheer.

The Holiday Claus is a holiday romance where a grumpy billionaire falls for his best friend's sunshine sister, wrapped in an age gap, only one bed spicy novella. This is a fast-paced, low drama, and light-hearted story meant to get you in the holiday spirit.

The Holiday Claus contains explicit sexual content, profanity, and mentions the death of a parent and an absentee parent.

Reading is meant to be your happy place—choose yourself, your needs, and your happiness first!

Xoxo,
Ann Einerson

*T'was the week before Christmas,
and her older brother's best friend was back in town.*

If Brooks didn't return,

this was the year he'd make his grandma frown.

*He moved to the big city,
forgetting all about his best friend's little sister.*

*But Lila never forgot about her not-so-little crush,
even if he was none the wiser.*

Oh no! What's this? A holiday wedding needs to be had.

Lila has just four days or risks the bride being sad.

Brooks and Lila will have to work together to get this couple wed.

Of course, at this little inn, there will be only one bed.

Brooks is a bit of a grump, but Lila is his secret ray of sunshine.

It won't be long until he looks into her eyes and says, "You're Mine."

The HOLIDAY Claus

PROLOGUE

ANOTHER GLANCE AT MY WATCH CONFIRMS I'M AN HOUR late.

This is just great.

Andrew's going to give me hell for being late to his engagement party, especially after he made it a point to remind me to be on time when we spoke on the phone earlier.

I take the last set of stairs two at a time, yanking my tie loose as I step out onto the rooftop terrace. The evening is cool for late August, and the air is filled with the soft chime of ice clinking in glasses and the chatter of mingling guests.

There's got to be at least a hundred people here. I'm tempted to leave since I'm not in the mood to socialize. Then again, I never am. I'd rather be at my office going through production schedules or at home sifting through the latest scripts my producers sent over.

I'm looking for the bar when Andrew shouts my name from across the terrace. He excuses himself from his conversation and heads my way, cutting off any chance of getting out of this.

"You're late," he remarks when he reaches me.

I shrug. "I had a work emergency."

Clara Victor, one of the A-list actresses at my studio, threw a fit over the director's script changes and threatened to walk if I didn't personally go to the film set to smooth things over. One setback of being the CEO of a movie studio means playing therapist, negotiator, and problem solver—even for actors who throw tantrums. Clara figured she had me wrapped around her finger— spoiler alert, she doesn't. Instead, I gave her an ultimatum: accept the director's revisions or be replaced. We're still in the early stages of production for the action film she's starring in, so we can look into recasting if necessary.

I don't have time for bullshit, certainly not from entitled celebrities who forget that everyone is replaceable. There's a reason why I avoid hooking up with talent under contract with SkyBound Studios or anyone in showbiz, for that matter. Managing their egos is a full-time job, without adding personal drama to the mix.

Andrew scoffs, folding his arms across his chest. "Oh, yeah? Well, my phone has gone off no less than fifteen times since the party started, but I promised Hannah I wouldn't work tonight."

I rub a hand over my face. Just the idea of ignoring a work call makes me anxious. "Want me to check if you have any urgent messages?" I offer.

"Nah." He dismisses me with a wave. "It's most likely a client wanting an update on an offer for their second mansion. It can wait. Hannah comes first, always."

I nod, pretending to understand. I'll never get how he can put business on the back burner so easily, particularly when dealing with high-profile clients. Still, despite his casual approach, Andrew is the most in-demand realtor for celebrities and wealthy individuals in Southern California.

We've been best friends since we were kids. He grew up in Starlight Pines, Vermont. My family spent every summer and Christmas there with our grandma, Kay, who owns Whispering Pines, the town's only inn.

Andrew and I both moved to California after we graduated high school and shared an apartment while I interned at a small production studio, and he worked at a coffee shop until he got his real estate license. Fifteen years later, we've both carved out successful careers—Andrew with his own real estate firm, and me as the owner and CEO of SkyBound Studios, the fastest-growing production company in the country.

He met his fiancée, Hannah, soon after moving here. Still, it took years for them to admit their feelings and even longer for him to propose. He's explained that's why she always comes first— he knows what life is like without her and refuses to take a single moment for granted.

As for me, I'm good with my life as it is—single, successful, and leaving the romance to the big screen.

Hannah joins us with a cheerful smile, her brown eyes sparkling with excitement. Andrew pulls her close and kisses her on the forehead.

"I'm so glad you made it, Brooks," she exclaims. "You showed up just in time to rescue me from a mind-numbing debate about the difference between glacier water and spring water. I thought I might actually fall asleep standing up." She sighs dramatically.

"Sounds goddamn awful," I grunt.

"Oh, it was," she confirms. "I'd rather listen to nails on a chalkboard than another group of Hollywood elites go on about how they can't live without their overpriced bottled water."

I nod in agreement. When I came to California, my focus was squarely on success, and I kept to myself. The higher a person climbs up the social ladder, the more insufferable the people around them become. Which is why Andrew and Hannah are practically the only ones I can tolerate being around.

"That's what I get for opening a yoga studio in downtown LA." Hannah sighs. "On the bright side, business is booming. Our waitlist is a mile long. It seems like everyone is looking for an alternative workout and a reprieve from the hustle and bustle of their hectic schedules." Andrew lightly nudges her, nodding toward me. "Sorry, Brooks, I didn't mean to talk your ear off."

"It's all good," I say with a tight smile. "I'm sure you have plenty of other guests to mingle with. I'll grab a drink and probably head out."

"You can't leave yet. You just got here." She offers me a piece of cardstock and a black pen, holding them out until I finally give in and take them.

"What's this for?" I ask skeptically.

"We're playing Bingo."

I shake my head and attempt to give the paper and pen back to her. "I'd rather not."

She raises a brow. "Too bad. Like you said, it's my engagement party, and as Andrew's best friend and future best man, you're obliged to participate," she says with a smirk.

I glance over at Andrew for backup, but he raises his hands in surrender. "Don't look at me," he says. "Hannah's the one running the show. What she says goes."

"Besides, it's not traditional Bingo. It's way more entertaining. Where's your sense of adventure?" Hannah nudges me playfully. "It won't hurt you to join in on the fun for once. Besides, Lila worked hard on planning this party and she would be devastated if she found out you didn't want to participate in the games she put together."

I turn to Andrew. "Lila...as in your sister, Lila?"

He nods. "Yeah. Usually, Hannah and I go back to Starlight Pines to see her and my parents, but I convinced her to come visit us for once. She offered to organize our engagement party while she was here."

Lila is eight years younger than Andrew and me. Most of my memories of her are of a kid with oversized glasses and an eager smile who wanted to be included in everything Andrew and I did.

The last time I saw her was over a decade ago, at a Christmas party at Whispering Pines Inn. She had braces and wore a red jumpsuit that made her stand out, even though it seemed like she was trying to blend in. I recall her shadowing my grandma, wanting to learn the ins and outs of running the inn. Now, Grandma tells me, Lila is the events planner there.

Andrew glances around the terrace. "Lila should be around here somewhere. I was hoping to give you two a chance to catch up."

"Last time I saw her, she was helping pass out the Bingo cards," Hannah chimes in, gesturing to the stack of them in her hands.

"Don't worry about it. Sounds like she's busy," I say.

Knowing Andrew, he'll rope me into playing chaperone for the night if I let him, and after the day I've had, the last thing I want is to be stuck trying to make small talk with someone I haven't seen in ages. Thankfully, before he can press me, a couple comes up to greet my newly engaged friends. I take it as my opportunity to step away, nodding to Andrew before heading in the opposite direction.

Usually, I steer clear of parties, preferring the solitude of my office or a quiet night at my penthouse apartment savoring a rare moment of peace. The only place I've ever felt a true sense of ease was Starlight Pines, but after my dad passed it was never the same. However, there was no getting out of this one, especially not since Andrew asked me to be his best man.

I wander along the perimeter of the rooftop in an effort to avoid conversation with the other guests. The place has been transformed into a tropical paradise, like one of my movie sets. Twinkling lights are wrapped around miniature palm trees, bamboo furniture is strategically placed to give those in attendance a place to relax. There's a tiki bar in the corner, and servers weave through the crowd, offering the guests piña coladas and passionfruit mojitos served in coconuts.

I notice a photo booth to my right, illuminated by a neon sign that reads *Love, Laughter, and Happily Ever After*. There's a giant basket of props on a nearby table, along with a corkboard filled with snapshots taken by the other guests.

When I look over to see Andrew and Hannah immersed in conversation with another couple, I relax my shoulders. If Hannah caught me standing here alone, she'd drag me into a photo op—props included.

I'm prepared to move on when I spot a manicured hand parting the photo booth curtain. A moment later, a woman peeks her head out. Her blonde hair tumbles in loose waves, while her sapphire eyes shine with a hint of mystery as she scans the crowd, furrowing her brow in concentration, oblivious to my presence.

I'm intrigued when she stiffens, her hand shooting to her mouth as she gasps at something across the rooftop. I follow her gaze to a man standing near the buffet. His hands are tucked in his pockets, scanning the area like he's searching for someone. The instant he looks in our direction, the woman yanks the curtain shut like she doesn't want to be found.

Normally, I'd mind my own business, but there's something captivating about her. Against my better judgment, I find myself wandering over to the photo booth and drawing back the curtain to get a closer look.

She snaps her head toward me, eyes wide with surprise. After a beat, she says, "Hi," her voice barely above a whisper.

When her gaze meets mine, I'm caught off guard by the unfamiliar warmth that sweeps over me. Her soft smile is disarming, making it impossible to look away.

From here I can make out the golden flecks in her irises, shimmering like sunlight dancing on rippling water. A smattering of freckles dusts the bridge of her nose, and her lips are full, parted slightly as she studies me in return. The sensible thing would be to close the curtain and give this woman her privacy, but I'm rooted to the spot. I've met plenty of attractive women, but I've never felt a magnetic pull like this before.

It's rather unnerving.

"I see you've turned the photobooth into your personal hideaway. Are you planning to camp out here all night?" I say, my curiosity peaked.

I have no business getting involved, but it grates on my nerves that I'm affected by a stranger who's only uttered a single syllable since I've been standing here.

The woman gives me a quick once-over and then peers past my shoulder out onto the rooftop. "I don't see anyone waiting for the photo booth unless you're referring to yourself. If that's the case, feel free to take a seat." She scoots over, patting the empty spot beside her, a faint blush creeping up her neck. "Can you make it quick, please?"

I take a better look around the photo booth. The inside is framed with dark wooden panels, and twinkle lights are draped across the wall opposite the vintage camera, creating a backdrop. The built-in bench is small, barely wide enough to fit two people.

Getting any closer is a bad idea, especially when a single glance from her causes my heart to race like it's going to pound right out of my chest.

"I'd rather not. Photo ops aren't my thing."

She scrunches her nose. "I see…and what exactly is your *thing*?" She emphasizes the last word with air quotes.

I start to speak but hesitate when she looks behind me again, and I instinctively follow her gaze to the man by the buffet. When he glances over, I hear the woman mumble under her breath, and I am taken by surprise when her slender fingers wrap around my arm. Her movements are quick and determined as she tugs me into the photo booth, and I grunt as I stumble inside the cramped space.

I'm aware of how close we are when she leans over to close the curtain. Her hair grazes my cheek, and the scent of peppermint and lavender fills the air, causing my pulse to quicken.

"Did you know frowning can increase stress levels? You really should smile more." She taps her finger against her chin, a playful glint forming in her eyes.

"Do you make it a habit of holding unwilling participants hostage in photo booths?" I deadpan.

If she were anyone else, I'd have already told her to get lost. Yet, this woman has completely disarmed me with that infectious smile of hers. I can't find it in me to be anything but intrigued, and I have to fight the grin threatening to break free.

Goddamn it.

I grit my teeth and shut my eyes to steady myself. If I had just minded my own business, I'd be at the bar, nursing a glass of scotch. Not being accosted by a charming woman hiding in a photo booth. I guess this is the price I pay for letting curiosity get the better of me.

After taking a deep breath, I open my eyes to find the mystery woman staring at me, her gaze soft yet curious.

"Let me guess, Bingo isn't your thing either?" she asks, dodging my earlier question.

I knit my brows together. "What?"

She motions to the Bingo card I didn't realize I was still holding. "It seemed like a fun icebreaker, but I forgot to check the prompts on the cards. That's what I get for ordering them online," she mutters, mostly to herself. "*Kiss another guest* wouldn't be a problem if I were married or in a relationship like everyone else here."

Certain I misheard her, I quickly glance at my Bingo card. I skim the prompts: take a selfie with the engaged couple; find someone who ordered the same drink; perform a dramatic reading of a romantic poem. Then, I spot it—kiss another guest.

Who the hell thought creating a Bingo card with these prompts was a good idea?

Although if I were trying to win the game, she'd be woman I'd choose to kiss while crossing off that square. My gaze tracks to her plump lips, and my imagination runs wild with the idea of running my tongue along the seams, coaxing her to kiss me.

I swallow, my throat tight. "Does this have something to do with why you're hiding out?" I motion to the Bingo card.

She nods. "Ricky, a guy who works at Hannah's yoga studio, kept going on about how we were the only single ones at the party, which, according to him, meant we were obligated to kiss if we wanted to mark off that square." She fiddles with the hem of her red floral dress. "I panicked and bolted when he turned his back to get a drink. When I saw the photo booth was empty, I slipped inside and figured I'd wait until the coast was clear before rejoining the party." She clasps her hands together in her lap.

"And you didn't kiss Ricky because…?" The question is out of my mouth before I can catch myself.

I've had the displeasure of meeting him a handful of times. He's the type who assumes every woman should swoon over him. He once tried asking Hannah out while they were closing the studio, but Andrew showed up, wrapping his arm around Hannah's waist and pulling her close to stake his claim. Ricky never dared flirt with her again.

"Call me old-fashioned, but I like to know a guy's last name before we go to first base." The woman's mouth twitches with amusement. "And taking me on a date wouldn't hurt either."

"I can't argue with that logic. It seems I'm already one step behind, given I still don't know your name."

Suddenly, I'm acutely aware of her thigh touching mine.

Damn, I haven't even had a drink, and yet I can barely think straight. It must be the lack of sleep from staying up all night re-viewing a contract because there's no way I'd normally be *this* distracted by an attractive woman. The voice in my head tells me to resist, but it's impossible to focus on anything other than the urge to close the gap between us.

It's no use.

When I look up, her eyes are heavy-lidded, staring at me with a silent plea. Her gaze darts to my mouth, her teeth skimming her lower lip.

I want to kiss this woman.

Hell, I *need* to kiss this woman…

She remains still as I cup her jaw, caressing her cheek. Her pupils grow wide as I lean in to brush my lips against hers in teasing strokes like I envisioned earlier. I groan when her hands land on my thighs, her fingers pressing into the fabric of my slacks. The touch sparks a flicker of desire that ignites within me like wildfire.

My body jolts forward, capturing her mouth in a possessive kiss. Her lush lips are smooth, glossy and taste like fresh strawberries. I let out a low growl when she opens her mouth to welcome me inside.

"Damn, I knew you'd taste sweet," I murmur.

As if emboldened by my words, she nips my bottom lip.

The last of my restraint snaps and I pull her over into my lap, her legs hanging to one side, and her dress rides up, as she settles against me, her body molded to mine. She shifts her hands to grip the nape of my neck.

My cock rubs against her ass, and she lets out a heady moan as she rocks into me. I'm pulsing with need, on the verge of giving her more, when a soft click followed by a sudden flash jolts me back to reality.

"What was that?" I ask.

I'm met with the woman's gaze as she studies me closely as

if gauging my reaction. Her hair is tousled from my grip, chest heaving like she's just run a marathon, and her pupils are dilated.

"I think that was—" Another click followed by the flash interrupts her. "The photo booth, taking our photo. It's programmed to take two at a time."

"Thank god, or we might have burned our retinas from that flash," I say, still blinking to clear my vision. "Doesn't this thing have a button you have to push for it to work?"

She shakes her head. "It's motion-activated, but I think the sensor's a little too sensitive," she says with a soft smile, a deep blush stains her cheeks.

The fact that our photo was taken during our kiss should bother me, but there's something more weighing on my mind.

"What's your name?" I ask.

Her smile slips, a shadow of disappointment crossing her face. "Lila," she whispers, pulling away just a bit.

That's when I spot the stack of Bingo cards on the bench seat next to her, and her earlier words replay in my head. *I forgot to check the prompts on the cards. That's what I get for ordering them online.*

Holy shit.

I just kissed my best friend's little sister…at his engagement party no less.

I'm left speechless, struggling to reconcile the fact that I didn't recognize Lila sooner. She's transformed from a shy teenager into a strikingly beautiful and self-confident woman. Her glasses are gone, giving me an unfiltered view of her striking blue eyes. And in place of her braces is a radiant smile, revealing perfectly straight teeth framed by those full, pouty lips. I catch myself wishing I could lean in and steal another kiss, just to see if the spark was a fluke or something more.

Seriously. What is wrong with me?

I gently set her down on the bench, needing to create space between us. "I should go."

Lila's smile falters, a brief flicker of dejection crosses her features before she quickly masks it. "Oh, okay. Well, it was nice to see you, Brooks."

I pause, staring at her in disbelief. "You remember me?" It hadn't occurred to me that she might, but it's oddly satisfying that she does.

She flashes me an infectious grin. "Of course I do. Your grandma talks about you and your brothers all the time. Plus, you haven't changed much since I saw you last." She pauses, tilting her head like she's studying me. "Well, aside from a few gray hairs and a more rigid posture," she teases, running her fingers along my temple.

I'm thrown off balance by the unexpected buzz of energy pulsing through me. Lila's breathing grows shallow as her gaze remains locked on mine, her hand lingering in my hair, and it makes me wonder if she feels the same undeniable pull between us.

Unable to resist, I trail my fingers along her arm in slow, deliberate strokes, savoring the warmth of her skin beneath my touch. The tension between us crackles like a live wire, the air thick with desire. My fingers itch to trace her jawline and explore the delicate curve of her neck as I tug her closer and claim her lips again.

She's your best friend's little sister, jackass.

My body stiffens as the reminder crashes over me like a bucket of cold water. I've already crossed one line; I can't cross another. Lila's the temptation I never saw coming, and now every second I hold back feels like I'm fighting a losing battle.

I draw in a sharp breath, bringing my hand to my side as I gather my resolve. "This shouldn't have happened." My tone is gruff, hiding the part of me that wishes she'd stay where she was.

Lila flinches, snatching her hand back.

A sharp pang of guilt tightens in my chest, but I push it aside. "I have to go."

"I understand. Goodbye, Brooks," she says, her shoulders slumping.

I scramble out of the photo booth, closing it behind me before I give in to my impulse and do something else we might regret.

I'm prepared to make a quick exit, but my plan is stalled when I see the pictures sitting in the outside slot. When a quick glance around confirms no one is watching, I grab the strip of photos and discreetly tuck it into my suit pocket for safekeeping.

Lila's comment about wanting a man to take her out lingers in my mind. I might be a moody son of a bitch, but for the chance to be with her, I'd tone it down for a night. I'd take her to the most expensive restaurant in the city and order their finest wine. A woman like her deserves nothing but the best. She also never said the date had to come before a kiss. So why do I feel bad for skipping out before giving her more?

I don't look back, worried I'll return to her if I do.

As I head toward the exit, my mind buzzes from the unexpected moment I just shared with her. My hand twitches from the memory of touching her. Thank god she lives on the other side of the country because I have a feeling that if I spent more time with her, all my restraint would go out the window. As it stands, I can return to my monotonous routine and pretend our encounter never happened.

CHAPTER 1

Lila

"**W**INSTON, PLEASE HURRY UP; IT'S FREEZING OUT HERE," I beg from my parents' back porch.

He pauses, tilting his head as if considering my plea before burying his nose back in the snow. His short legs keep sinking into the deep drifts, but that doesn't stop him from digging with single-minded focus, ignoring the cold and my attempts to coax him inside. He's a master of selective hearing unless peanut butter biscuits are involved.

I sigh, tugging my coat tighter around me, waiting for him to finish. While most dachshunds shy away from the snow, Winston treats it like his personal playground, undeterred by the bitter cold or the fact that the snow is almost as tall as he is.

I'm momentarily distracted from the chilly conditions when my phone chimes in my pocket.

A smile tugs at my lips when I see Fallon's name pop up on the screen. She's a private chef I met a few years back when clients flew her in to cater their wedding at Whispering Pines Inn, where

I work as an event planner. We hit it off right away, and despite living in different places, we've stayed close ever since.

Fallon: Remind me why I thought moving to New York was a good idea?

Lila: Because you were tired of living in London and wanted a new adventure.

Fallon: As my best friend, it's your job to stop me from making impulsive decisions.

Lila: How could I forget? Next time I'll be sure to hop on a flight to remind you in person to think twice before moving to a different country.

Fallon: Now that's more like it.

Fallon: How're the holidays with your fam?

Lila: Great! You know I love this time of year!

Lila: Andrew and Hannah flew in yesterday, so I'm spending the day with them before I have to work through Christmas, handling a wedding party that arrives tomorrow.

Fallon: Have you thought any more about moving? You could always join me in New York and we can make questionable choices together.

Fallon: Or what about Southern California? With Andrew and Hannah's connections, you could easily start your own event planning company out there.

I've been toying with the idea of moving for a while, but Starlight Pines is home, and the notion of starting over somewhere else is daunting. Besides, Kay Claus, the inn's owner and a grandmother figure to me, had a health scare last month. I can't bring myself to leave her alone to manage things on her own.

I live in a small cottage behind the inn, and aside from managing the events, I assist her with upkeep, running errands, and anything else she needs.

Lila: I can't leave Starlight Pines right now, but I'm not ruling out moving sometime next year.

Fallon: I'll hold you to it! You deserve to have an adventure of a lifetime.

Lila: Oh, like you're doing in New York?

Fallon: Touché

Fallon: Omg! I forgot to tell you about my date last night. I couldn't get out of there fast enough when he mentioned he lives with his mother and owns a pet tarantula.

Lila: I thought you were all about having an adventure?

Fallon: Are you saying you'd be fine sleeping in the same room as a giant hairy spider?

I shiver at the idea of it. Who the heck keeps a spider as a pet, or better yet thinks it's a good conversation piece? News flash: It's not.

Lila: Heck no! I'd run for the hills.

Fallon: My point exactly.

Before I can put my phone away, a notification pops up, alerting me to a new work email. I frown when I notice it's from Frankie, the bride set to get married on Christmas, which is only four days from now.

The wedding party is set to arrive tomorrow afternoon. They rented a large cabin nearby since the majority of the rooms at the inn had been booked out for more than a year. Holiday weddings, in particular, are popular at the inn, and we've had at least one every year since I started working there.

Weddings and Christmas are two of my favorite things. Nothing compares to a bride walking down the aisle surrounded by winter wonderland décor, with snowflakes falling outside the window as she and the groom exchange vows.

My shoulders slump as I skim the email. Frankie and her fiancé have decided to postpone their wedding, opting for a summer wedding in the Hamptons. She says her father already wired over the full amount they owe—which I guess isn't a problem when he's a pharmaceutical executive and money is no object. That doesn't erase the disappointment washing over me and the sting when I realize three months of preparation have gone down the drain.

Winston's barking interrupts my pity party. He's pawing at the back door and whines impatiently when I don't move fast enough.

I can't help but laugh at his newfound urgency. "Oh, so now you want to go in?" He barks again, and I roll my eyes at his theatrics. "Okay, okay, I'm coming," I assure him as I open the door.

He barrels inside, bypassing the kitchen, and zooms down the hall, disappearing into the front living room. Once I remove my shoes and hang up my coat, I follow after him.

When I get there, I'm welcomed by the warmth of the crackling fire. My parents are curled up on the plaid couch, and Andrew and Hannah are seated on cushions across from them. They're all gathered around the coffee table, where a game of Scrabble is in progress. The Christmas tree we decorated last night is set up in the corner, adorned with twinkling lights, strings of popcorn, and red and white ornaments.

Andrew and Hannah don't visit as often as they'd like, but they always make it a priority to spend the holidays in Starlight Pines with my parents and me. Now that they're engaged, it's even more special to have them here.

I can't suppress the flicker of envy that creeps in. For the past seven years, I've helped brides from all over the country plan their dream weddings at Whispering Pines. Most of my childhood friends are now married and have moved away. Even my brother, who once swore he'd never settle down, has found his perfect match, begging the question if I'm destined to be forever the wedding planner and never the bride. A pang of remorse washes over me for letting my insecurities overshadow my excitement for Andrew and Hannah, knowing they deserve all the happiness in the world.

I notice that Winston has made himself at home next to my mom, devouring a peanut butter biscuit she must have had waiting for him. He wags his tail happily, ignoring my presence. You'd think I'd be his favorite since I let him sleep in bed with me, give him daily belly rubs, and replace his favorite toy hippo whenever he chews it to pieces. Instead, his loyalty shifts to whoever showers him with the most attention. *Traitor.*

My mom is a strong contender for his favorite person. She spoils him with his favorite snacks, keeps a ramp next to the couch for when he comes to visit, and makes him an impressive selection of sweaters. The blue and white one he's wearing now, complete with hand-stitched reindeer, is proof that she treats him like her four-legged grandchild. And Winston isn't shy about using that to his advantage.

My dad places his last tile on the board and jots down his score in his pocket-sized notepad. When he's finished with his turn, he pushes his wire-framed glasses up his nose and looks at me. "We're almost done, kiddo. You can take my spot for the next game," he says.

I fold my arms across my chest. "That's okay, Dad. I'd rather watch."

He rubs his chin. "But you love Scrabble," he reminds me. "And you might not get another chance to play before Christmas since you'll be so busy working."

The reminder has me exhaling deeply, and I pull my arms closer around myself. I can't help but be let down by Frankie's canceled wedding. Even though I'm still getting paid and should be thrilled about having more time with my family this holiday season, it's hard not to think all the work I put in was for nothing.

"Is something bothering you, Lila?" my mom asks, her voice gentle.

Everyone in the room looks in my direction, waiting for me to answer.

I run a hand through my hair and drop my gaze to the floor. "I just got an email from the bride who's supposed to be getting married on Christmas day telling me she's decided to—" I'm interrupted mid-sentence by the chime of the doorbell.

My dad frowns. "Are we expecting someone?" he asks my mom.

"That's probably Brooks," Andrew interjects. "He's in town to visit his grandma. I told him to grab a rideshare from the airport and get dropped off here, so we can drive him to the inn since it's out of the way." He turns to me. "Lila, could you let him in?"

Brooks is here?

My gaze darts to the door, and my heart skips a beat at the possibility. Kay hasn't said anything about him or his brothers visiting, and I'm sure she would have told me if she knew they were coming. My hands grow clammy, and butterflies swarm in my stomach as the memory of Brooks and me squeezed into the photo booth at Andrew and Hannah's engagement party drifts through my mind. Four months later, and it feels like a distant dream, a mere figment of my imagination.

I blink, slightly dazed when I hear Andrew's voice. "Sorry, what did you say?"

He lifts a brow. "Brooks is at the door. Can you let him in?"

A warm blush spreads across my cheeks. "Yeah, of course."

I move to the entryway on autopilot, my hands clasped tightly at my sides.

Winston is already there, his tail wagging with excitement, eager to greet whoever is here. He probably thinks it's the mailman who always brings him a treat. Winston made it clear early on that he'll gladly accept peanut butter biscuits or chicken treats in exchange for not barking his head off whenever he sees the mailman at my parents' house or the inn.

My heart pounds in my ears while I hesitantly reach for the handle.

It's not a big deal. I'm just about to face the guy I've had a crush on since I was twelve and kissed in a photo booth the last time we crossed paths. Totally normal, right?

You can do this.

The mantra plays on repeat in my head as I attempt to bolster my confidence. Despite my best efforts, my knees are unsteady, and I wish the idea of seeing Brooks again didn't ignite old feelings I thought I'd buried years ago. Apparently, there's no stopping a childhood crush from resurfacing, no matter how much time has passed.

Another knock echoes through the house, and I steady myself with a deep breath before opening the door.

Brooks Claus stands on my parents' front porch, his tall frame filling the doorway. His tailored charcoal suit molds to his broad shoulders and the stern line of his mouth emphasizes the sharpness of his jaw.

He's more handsome than I remember.

I manage a nervous smile. "Hey, Brooks."

He gives me a curt nod. "Lila." His cold greeting leaves me momentarily speechless, the silence growing more awkward by the second.

"Are you going to let me in, or should I stay out here and freeze?" he asks, leaning against the doorframe.

I swallow hard, caught off guard by his bluntness. "Right, sorry." I move aside, motioning for him to come in.

Winston barks sharply when Brooks steps into the entryway, his disappointment clear that it's not the mailman. He circles Brooks with the confidence of a ruler sizing up his subject.

Brooks drops his carry-on against the wall and scowls at him. "Great, a dog with an attitude," he mutters.

"His name is Winston," I correct him.

"Does he make a habit of acting like he runs the place?"

I put my hands on my hips. "For your information, he's an excellent judge of character, and it's obvious he's unimpressed by you."

Winston releases a dramatic huff, casting Brooks a skeptical glare as if to say he agrees this guy isn't worth his time before trotting into the living room with an indignant flick of his tail.

"Brooks, glad you made it, man," my brother calls from the living room.

I shut the front door and follow behind Brooks, watching

as my entire family greets him. My mom gets up and pulls him into a big hug, unfazed by his stiff posture. He used to spend as much time at our house as he did at the inn during his visits in the summer and over the holidays, and my parents consider him one of their own.

Once we're all seated, my mom turns to me. "Lila, what was it you were trying to tell us earlier?"

Everyone looks in my direction—including Brooks.

"The Christmas wedding we had booked at the inn has been canceled. The bride decided at the last minute she'd rather get married in the Hamptons this summer."

My mom's eyes soften with understanding. "I'm sorry to hear that, honey. Have you canceled with all the vendors?"

I shake my head. "Not yet. Thankfully, the bride's father paid for the wedding in full, so everyone will be compensated."

Usually, I coordinate directly with the vendors, allowing the brides to communicate exclusively with me regarding their wedding plans.

"The inn is the perfect setting for a Christmas wedding," my mom says. "It's a pity there won't be one there this year." She shifts her gaze to Andrew and Hannah. "Don't you two agree?" Her tone is deceptively casual.

What is she up to?

It's no secret that she's disappointed they haven't set a date or picked a venue for their wedding yet. I can understand, considering it's been a long time coming.

Andrew met Hannah shortly after he moved to California. They remained friends for nearly a decade before Hannah admitted her feelings and gave Andrew an ultimatum: either choose to take the next step or let her go. They've been together ever since, and our family was elated when he finally proposed three months ago.

Andrew sighs. "Mom, we've talked about this, remember? Hannah and I will decide on a date when we're ready."

Hannah rests a hand on his arm. "The inn is gorgeous this time of year with its snow-covered trees and twinkling lights everywhere. It would make for the perfect romantic winter wedding, don't you think? Our wedding," she adds tentatively, watching him closely.

Andrew's expression shifts from contemplation to a warm smile. "It's a great location, but I figured you'd want to get married in California."

Hannah shakes her head. "Honestly, no. Between your hectic work schedule and trying to coordinate our ever-changing guest list, it's been impossible to set a date that works for everyone. Our engagement party was lovely, but it felt more like a networking event for co-workers and industry professionals than something that was just for us." She pauses, giving his hand a squeeze. "I don't want to wait any longer to be your wife, and the most important people in our lives are in this room." She motions toward Brooks, my parents, and me. "What do you say, Drew? Marry me at Whispering Pines Inn on Christmas?"

Hannah is an only child and doesn't have a relationship with her parents. So, over the years, our family has become hers.

Andrew leans in to kiss her on the forehead, a grin tugging at the corner of his mouth. "Anything for you, babe."

My mom claps her hands together. "My goodness. This is the best news. Don't you agree, Ryan?" She turns to my dad.

He chuckles. "Yes, dear, it's great news."

"What do you think, Lila? Can you put together a new wedding in four days?" Hannah asks, a hopeful smile crossing her face. "I'm sure we can use the majority of the decorations and activities you've already planned for the original wedding."

I run a hand across my face at the realization. I was so caught up in the excitement about them finally setting a date that I forgot about the logistics. I've planned hundreds of weddings, but never on such short notice. It's a good thing I haven't reached out to cancel with the vendors yet, so in theory, I could repurpose the existing plans to pull this off. However, I'd never want Hannah to feel like she's settling for anything less than her dream wedding.

I rest my hand over my heart. "I'd be honored to plan your wedding on one condition. This is your special day, and we're going to make sure it's tailored to your preferences the best we can on short notice. Whatever you want, we'll make it happen."

"Thank you, Lila," she exclaims. "Will you be my maid of honor? There's no one else I'd rather have by my side on the most important day of my life."

A lump forms in my throat, but I still manage to say, "I'd love to."

She is like the sister I never had, and being a part of her big day is a privilege I'll cherish forever. Andrew won the lottery when he found her, and I can't wait to help make their big day unforgettable.

"This is great," Andrew chimes in. "I've already asked Brooks to be my best man, so he can help you with wedding prep. He's staying at the inn, so it'll be convenient."

Brooks arches a brow. "Oh right, because wedding prep is totally in my wheelhouse."

"Why not? You've got the experience running a whole studio, so planning a wedding should be a breeze."

"Managing multimillion-dollar movies is a whole different ballgame than coordinating a wedding."

"Oh, come on," Andrew prods. "You could do it with your eyes closed."

I put a hand on my hip and shoot my brother a glare. "It's not that easy. There are guests to contact, decor to find. Not to mention favors to wrap and—"

Andrew cuts me off, turning to Brooks. "See, she needs your help."

Brooks shakes his head. "It's really not a good idea. Lila is the professional here," he says, gesturing toward me without looking at me. "The last thing she needs is me getting in the way. Besides, I'm scheduled to fly back to California tomorrow."

"What for? You said filming wrapped yesterday for the last project until the New Year. Anything urgent, you can handle when you have some downtime," Andrew suggests.

Brooks glances my way, his hesitation palpable, before redirecting his attention to Andrew. "Fine, but only because you're twisting my arm," he grumbles.

I wince at his response; his words hurt more than they should. It's apparent his reluctance is because of me.

I'm not sure what I expected when I saw him again, but reluctance wasn't it. Now I'm wondering if I romanticized our brief encounter in the photo booth. Was I just clinging to an old teenage crush that was nothing more than an illusion? It's painfully obvious that Brooks isn't exactly thrilled to be here, let alone help me with wedding prep.

I'd be wise to remember that if he does stay in Starlight Pines for the wedding, it'll be out of obligation to my brother—not because of the connection we shared at the engagement party. Thinking otherwise would be naive. To Brooks, it was likely nothing more than a fleeting lapse in judgment that he's long since forgotten.

Kay likes to say that the holiday season is magical, but I'm beginning to think that's just wishful thinking, dressed up in tinsel and good intentions. Yet, a small part of me still clings to the hope that this year will be different, and that the spirit of Christmas will work its magic after all.

CHAPTER 2

Brooks

"LOOKS LIKE YOU'RE STICKING AROUND LONGER THAN YOU expected," Andrew states. "There's no chance my best man is skipping out on my wedding."

"Guess I don't have much of a choice, do I?" I reply, feigning reluctance.

"Nope," he says with a smirk.

My original plan was to check on Grandma and fly back to California tomorrow. The holidays aren't exactly my favorite time of year, and I've managed to avoid celebrating them until now. But between Andrew's Christmas wedding and my grandma's love for the season, there's no escaping it this year.

Andrew's still talking about the wedding, but I'm having trouble focusing on what he's saying, distracted by the sweet smell of peppermint and lavender wafting through the air, causing me to clench my jaw. It's the same scent that's been etched in my memory for the past four months, despite my efforts to erase it.

I should have known better than to stop by the Monroes' place. The plan was to go straight from the airfield to the inn, but when Andrew found out I was coming to town, he suggested I have my rideshare drop me off at his parents' and he would drive me the rest of the way since Whispering Pines Inn is a ways out of town.

The last thing I expected was for Lila to answer the door. Her leggings hugged her curves, and her doe-eyes lit up when she saw me. My fingers itched to trace her collarbone when I noticed that her sweater had slipped off one shoulder, revealing a glimpse of her creamy skin.

She's more beautiful than I remember.

Running a renowned film production studio means that I'm not easily rattled. I'm frequently challenged with high-stakes decisions and have learned to stay composed, even when everything is on the line. I'm laser-focused on my business, leaving no room for distractions.

Until now.

I've been haunted by flashes of Lila's smile and her lyrical laughter echoing in my mind for the past four months. The worst part is I've rejected every woman I've had the chance to spend the night with since then, unable to shake the feeling that none of them would compare to her. It's absurd that after spending only a few minutes with Lila, and kissing in a photo booth, it's become impossible to think about anyone else.

"Brooks, are you coming?" Andrew waves a hand in front of my face to grab my attention.

I blink several times. "Where are we going?"

He shakes his head with a chuckle. "We're going to Whispering Pines so Lila can show us her vision for the event space and get the rundown of how we can help prepare for the wedding." I glance around, noticing the rest of his family gathered by the entryway waiting on us.

When I join them my eyes immediately find Lila. She's sitting on the bottom step of the stairs, bent over to slip on her boots. I bite back a grin when I notice the reindeer on her socks and the candy cane pattern on her leggings. It's evident by her wardrobe choice that she loves the holidays.

My fingers flex at my side when her shirt rides up, revealing a sliver of skin. The image of one hand on her hip, pulling her flush against me, as I run my other through her sun-kissed hair, tipping her chin up to meet my gaze, peppering kisses along her jawline plays through my mind.

What the hell was that?

"Brooks, you can ride with Hannah and me." I whip my head around to see Andrew heading out the front door.

"I'm coming." I grab my suitcase and follow after him.

God, that was a close call…way too close. I've only been in the same room with Lila for five minutes and I'm already finding it challenging to keep my self-control in check.

I'd do well to remember that she's only twenty-five—eight years younger than me. She lives on the other side of the country, and chances are her family wouldn't be too pleased if they knew I had any interest beyond helping her with the wedding.

Here's to hoping the car ride to the inn will give me the space I need to clear my head.

Whispering Pines Inn hasn't changed much since I was here last. Rustic wooden beams stretch across the ceiling, wrapped with garlands of pine and holly, and wreaths with red ribbons hang from every doorway, adding a festive touch to the space. The lobby's floor-to-ceiling windows showcase a panoramic view of the serene lake and mountains in the distance.

A group of guests is gathered by a table across the room, where a pitcher of apple cider and a plate of gingerbread cookies are set out. Several people have moved to the seating area, complete with leather chairs and couches positioned around a grand fireplace. Its mantle is decorated with twined evergreen garlands strung with cranberries and bells.

The embroidered stockings my grandma made for my brothers and me are hanging from the hearth. My eyes drift to the one on the end with a train on the front. Grandma made it for my dad when he was a kid. Christmas was his favorite holiday, and it feels like just yesterday when we were here together, hanging lights and decorating the inn for the holidays, Grandma rewarding us with hot chocolate and homemade biscotti when we finished.

Lila's melodic laugh breaks through my gloomy thoughts. She's next to the reception desk, where she's speaking with family discussing wedding prep.

She's in a pink coat that matches her energy, effortlessly lighting up the room. Her blonde hair is loosely braided, a few wisps framing her face, and I fight the urge to cross the room and tuck them behind her ear.

"Brooks, what a pleasant surprise." Grandma steps into the lobby, holding a fresh plate of gingerbread cookies. After adding them to the refreshment table, she comes to greet me, pulling me in for a tight hug.

"Why didn't you tell me you were coming to visit?" she asks.

A fresh wave of guilt washes over me for avoiding this place for so long. Until now, I've only been back once since my dad died. It felt like reopening an old wound that I wasn't ready to face.

"When were you planning to tell me or Jameson you were sick?" I ask point-blank. "We talk on the phone every week, yet you conveniently failed to mention you were hospitalized last month after experiencing chest pain and shortness of breath."

"I should have known better than to let Lila talk me into going to a fancy cardiologist in the city, who would go and tattle to your brother," she mutters.

Jameson is coming out on Christmas Eve but asked if I could check on her sooner. Our younger brother, Calder, is on one of his extreme adventures, scaling mountains in Nepal. He's off the grid until the New Year, making him unreachable, which leaves me to handle things on my own until Jameson arrives.

The truth is I'm not sure if I ever would have come back if it hadn't been for Grandma's health scare.

"You're making a big deal out of nothing," she adds after a beat. "I'm doing much better now, so there's no need to worry," she replies with a wave of her hand.

I shoot her a skeptical glance. "Grandma, you had a heart attack. That's not something you can brush off like it's nothing."

"A *mild* heart attack," she corrects me. "The doctor said as long as I take it easy, I have nothing to worry about."

"And you consider running an inn on your own, taking it easy?"

She scoffs. "Please. I have Lila."

I furrow my brow. "She's just the event planner."

Grandma playfully squeezes my cheek. "Oh honey, she's my right hand. I couldn't do this without her."

"What do you mean?"

"Aside from event planning, she handles everything from bookkeeping to managing the staff. Remember how she used to run around here, always eager to help out?" Grandma asks. "Well, now she does. Some days I think she's got it figured out better than I do. But she has other aspirations, I just wish she'd share them with me. Still, she takes such good care of me and the inn."

Regret settles in my chest as her words sink in. I should have put my grandma first, instead of my own discomfort over being back here. It's not right that she's had to rely on someone other than my brothers and I to take on the role of helping her.

I don't expect the added guilt I feel for letting Lila take on this responsibility alone. Although I wasn't aware of the extent of her involvement in looking after my grandma, I should have paid closer attention.

Grandma raised my dad on her own, and now that he's gone, my brothers and I are the only family she has left. Although she's made trips to visit us all, Starlight Pines is her home, and nothing would make her happier than to have all her grandsons under one roof again—even if just for a visit like the ones we shared growing up.

It's hard to say if that'll ever happen. Losing Dad hit us all hard, and we each found our own way to cope. We didn't talk about it much, and over time, we drifted apart.

Jameson poured his soul into medical school, specializing in pediatric surgery. He thinks that if he can give his young patients a fighting chance at survival, it might somehow quiet the emptiness he's been carrying.

Calder has distanced himself by traveling, drifting from country to country. He calls to check in every few months, but I haven't seen him in person since the Christmas after Dad passed.

As for me, I dove headfirst into my career. It was the easiest way to distract from the pain of losing Dad and the shame of avoiding Starlight Pines.

Out of the corner of my eye, I notice a guy around my age, with annoyingly perfect hair approach the reception desk. He taps Lila on the shoulder to get her attention, and she turns around, greeting him with a broad smile. When he starts to speak, she leans in, listening intently.

Damn, I wish I could hear what they were saying.

My grandma clears her throat, her gaze following mine to the reception desk. "Funny, I don't remember you being this interested in the front desk when you used to visit," she teases with a smirk.

I snap my head in her direction. "I'm not," I insist, feeling my cheeks warm under her scrutiny, hoping she'll drop it.

"Whatever you say," she says skeptically. "I really am glad

you're here. Although I wish you would have told me you were coming sooner. How long do I have you?"

"It was going to be for the night, but now that Andrew and Hannah decided to have their wedding this coming weekend, looks like I'm yours until the day after Christmas."

"How nice of my grandson to spare some time for his grandma," she says, with an exaggerated sigh.

"I didn't mean it that way."

"Don't get your feathers ruffled, I'm only teasing. I understand your reasons for staying away for so long." She runs her fingers along the blue pendant necklace my dad gave her. "The only problem is, I gave the last available room to a lovely couple who's spending their honeymoon in the area, and no other guests are checking out until after the New Year."

"Well, shit," I mutter.

The closest hotel is fifty miles away, and Andrew's parents now have relatives coming into town for the wedding, so I can't stay at their place.

Grandma playfully smacks my arm. "Don't make me pull out the swear jar," she warns. "You've got the money to fill it now, but Santa might just save a trip and bring you coal."

"Pretty sure I'm already on the naughty list." I chuckle, stopping short when she swats my arm again.

She might be small in stature, but her presence commands respect, and she knows exactly how to use it to her advantage.

"Who's staying in the cottage?" I ask, deciding it's best to change the subject.

When my dad helped Grandma expand the inn, he made sure one was built at the back of the property so she could have some privacy. However, she refused to move in, preferring to stay in the cramped innkeeper's quarters near the main entrance so she could personally greet the guests and be close by if they needed anything.

"Lila and Winston live there," Grandma states matter-of-factly. "When I hired Lila, she commuted from her parents' house but was looking for a place of her own. Since I rarely booked out the cottage, I suggested she stay there. It's been a tremendous blessing having her so close. I expect you to behave yourself and not stir up any trouble while you're here." She wags her finger at me. "Lila has been my constant, and I consider her family. Whatever you do, make sure you treat her right, or you'll have to answer to me, got it?"

"You're worried for nothing," I say, trying to reassure her. "I'm just here to visit you and to support Andrew. That's it."

Even I don't find that convincing.

"Is that so?" Grandma asks skeptically. "Then care to explain why you didn't tell me you ran into Lila during his engagement party."

"How did you know about that?"

She beams at me. "Lila mentioned it. And now you're in Starlight Pines, unable to keep your eyes off her. What do you think I should make of that?"

I sigh, rubbing at my temples. "I mean it. There's nothing happening between Lila and me."

"Whatever you say, dear," Grandma says, patting me on the arm with a knowing look that suggests she's not buying it for a second. "Now, about the sleeping arrangements. I rearranged the storage room last week, and there's a cot in there you can use. It's not one of those fancy presidential suites you're used to, but it's all I've got, so you'll have to make do."

I stare at her, hoping I heard her wrong. "You want me to sleep in the storage room?"

She nods enthusiastically. "It'll be far more comfortable than the limited space in my room," she assures me.

Well, this is just great.

Despite my lack of enthusiasm, I manage a small smile. "Thanks, Grandma. I appreciate it."

The last thing she needs is to deal with my sour mood. The whole point of my visit is to make sure she's well taken care of, and I don't want to add to her worries. I can handle a little discomfort for her sake.

I frown when I hear a whining sound and am confused when I spot Lila's dog, Winston, sitting at my grandma's feet. As soon as she looks down, he rises to his hind legs and swipes his front paws in the air.

Grandma claps her hands like he's just performed the trick of a lifetime. "Winn, you're too much." She chuckles as he yips, pawing the air again. "Not to worry, I have a special treat for you." She pulls a Christmas tree-shaped dog biscuit from her apron pocket, and Winston eagerly takes it from her outstretched hand, wolfing it down like his life depends on it and licking his chops when he's finished.

"Do you think it's wise to reward him for that kind of behavior?" I inquire.

Winston whips his head in my direction, shooting me a sharp glare for daring to intervene with his snack time. With a flick of his tail, he turns back to Grandma, nudging his head against her leg, effectively dismissing me.

She leans down to scratch him behind the ear. "Don't listen to him, Winn. You deserve as many treats as you want," she says in a sing-song voice.

I roll my eyes. "Why does it seem like you're choosing a side, and I'm somehow losing to the dog?"

"Don't take it personally," Lila chimes in, strolling over to stand next to me. "Winston has had your grandma wrapped around his paw since the first time they met, and I'm afraid you'll have to settle for second place."

"Nonsense, Lila. You're my second favorite by far. Maybe

someone would rank higher if he actually showed up to visit me on occasion," Grandma says, casting me a mock-serious look.

"Glad to know whose side you're on," I mutter just as Winston looks up and gives me a low growl. "I think your dog needs to work on his manners."

"Oh, please." Lila shakes her head, laughing softly. "Winston loves everyone, even the mailman. It must be your grumpy disposition that rubs him the wrong way," she quips. "That or the fact that you haven't offered him a single treat. He *loves* treats."

Winston barks, spinning in circles at the sound of what must be his favorite word.

"No need to get yourself in a tizzy, Winn," Grandma says. "Let's go to the kitchen and get you another biscuit." She walks away with Winston padding after her. "Please do try to behave yourself, Brooks," she calls over her shoulder.

Unbelievable.

I shouldn't be surprised she has a soft spot for Lila—who wouldn't, with those big blue eyes and her bright outlook? Winston isn't the only one acting differently around me. After the photo booth incident, I'd hoped Lila would be happy to see me. Then again, my abrupt exit after we shared an explosive kiss might explain why she's acting like she'd rather be anywhere else.

If you weren't such a jackass, maybe she'd be more excited to see you.

Clearly, my conscience has no problem calling me out.

"Where'd your family go?" I ask Lila, noticing they're no longer in the lobby.

"They went back to my parents' place. My aunt Tilly is driving down from New Hampshire, so Mom wanted to get the guest room ready before she arrives. Andrew saw you talking with your grandma and didn't want to interrupt. He said he'd catch you tomorrow morning at the gym and back here in the afternoon for the day's wedding festivities. Here's the full itinerary."

She hands me a piece of cardstock with Andrew & Hannah's names in golden script across the top, the paper still warm from the printer. I skim through the activities listed leading up to the wedding day. Every day is jam-packed with events.

"When did you have time to put this together?" I ask, holding up the itinerary.

"You'd be surprised what I can pull off when I'm on a deadline. I kept some of the activities I originally planned but added a few that I know Andrew and Hannah would enjoy, like the sleigh ride." She taps on the highlighted item.

"You're really pulling out all the stops, huh?" I nod toward the itinerary. "What's next? A life-sized ice sculpture of the happy couple?"

When Andrew and Hannah decided to get married this coming weekend, I didn't anticipate a full schedule. I figured I'd be assigned a few quick tasks leading up to the Christmas wedding but could spend most of the time catching up on work. This detailed schedule is far more than I bargained for.

Not to mention, with a packed itinerary, Lila's going to require extra help. My resolve is already hanging by a thread, and there's no telling what could happen if we're stuck in close quarters for too long.

She lifts her chin, meeting my gaze head-on. "Listen, Brooks, I know that you'd rather be anywhere else other than stuck helping me. And if you're only going to make things harder, I'd rather you didn't help at all." She plucks the itinerary from my hand and slips it back into her binder. "This wedding has to go off without a hitch, and I refuse to let you get in the way."

Panic coils in my stomach as she begins to walk away. "Lila, wait." I catch her wrist, and she turns around, meeting my gaze with a guarded expression. It bothers me that she's retreated into herself, and more than anything, I want to see her smile again.

"What is it?" she asks.

"I didn't mean to make things harder for you. What you're doing for Andrew and Hannah is incredible, and I shouldn't have been so dismissive." I rake a hand through my hair, briefly glancing at the ground before meeting her inquisitive gaze. "I've never planned a wedding before, but it's obvious it's an enormous undertaking to organize one in such short order. I'd still like to help you if you'll have me."

"Last I checked, you were more interested in arguing than wedding planning," she counters, hugging her binder to her chest.

"Fair point," I admit. "But if you're willing, I'd like another chance. I promise I'll be on my best behavior." I extend my arm for a handshake. "Do we have a deal?" I add when she doesn't respond right away.

I'm beginning to think she's going to reject my apology, but after what feels like an eternity, she places her hand in mine.

"Deal," she says. The hint of a smile she offers is like an addictive drug.

The softness of her skin against my rough palm has me absentmindedly grazing my thumb across her wrist. Her breath hitches as her eyes stay locked on mine. The familiar urge to kiss her slips into my mind like it has nearly every day since the night of the engagement party.

That's when I see my grandma near the reception desk watching us, an amused twinkle in her eye.

I blink rapidly, pulling my hand back to my side. "I have to make a few calls and notify my team I won't be back in California until after Christmas. I'll be free to help you with wedding preparations tomorrow," I inform her, spinning around and hightailing it out of the lobby without giving Lila a chance to reply.

I've only been in town a few hours, and I'm already in danger of crossing lines I shouldn't.

So why does it feel impossible not to?

CHAPTER 3

Lila

I PRESS MY FACE INTO MY PILLOW WHEN MY ALARM GOES OFF at the crack of dawn, wishing for a few more minutes of sleep. I'm far from an early bird, but with only three days left to pull off Andrew and Hannah's wedding, an early start is unavoidable.

If I'd gone to bed at a decent hour, maybe I wouldn't be fighting to keep my eyes open.

After talking with Brooks last night, Winston and I came back to our cottage, where I worked on a tentative seating chart for the wedding. It's going to be an intimate event, primarily with friends from town and a handful of relatives who can make the trip at the last minute.

I'm still unsure about having Brooks help. There's a constant tug-of-war inside me with him being back in Starlight Pines. I can't shake the memory of our time together at the engagement party, the intensity of his gaze, the scent of his cologne, and the feel of his hair, and the light scrape of his scruff against my fingers. It replays in my mind like a film stuck on repeat, each frame sharper than the last. And now with him back in town, it's hard to separate the past from the present. The lines are beginning to blur, and I'm powerless to stop it.

I groan when my alarm goes off again, reminding me to get a move on. Sitting up in bed, I grab my phone and see a message from Fallon.

Fallon: Would you bail me out of jail if I were arrested???

Lila: Depends on the charges. If it's for jaywalking, you're on your own. I don't condone petty crimes.

Fallon: What about breaking a hockey stick over someone's head?

Fallon: I can assure you it would totally be justified.

Lila: That's suspiciously specific. Does this have something to do with Harrison?

Fallon: I plead the fifth.

Lila: I better start planning your alibi.

Fallon: And this is why you're my emergency contact. You have my back, no questions asked.

Lila: Please tell me how you expect to live under the same roof as him without any casualties?

Fallon: Thankfully, I have some time to plan my survival strategy since he's leaving tonight to spend the holidays with his family in Aspen Grove.

Fallon: Except he's left me with his demon cat and insists it has free reign over his apartment.

Fallon: I swear this thing is feral.

Lila: Oh gosh, I'd give anything to watch you try and tame him.

Fallon: I swear it's part gremlin.

She moved to New York six months ago but was recently evicted from the basement apartment she was renting. Her landlord unexpectedly decided to sell their brownstone, and unfortunately, Fallon had a hard time finding a new place to live in the city on such short notice.

Last month, she temporarily moved in with Harrison Stafford, one of her new clients. He has a penthouse apartment in New York City with plenty of space. However, it doesn't sound like either of them is happy about the arrangement.

When I pressed Fallon about moving in with someone she barely knows and isn't particularly fond of, she revealed that she'd met him back when she was in culinary school. She had catered an event for the Rangers, the professional hockey team Harrison used to play for. They went on a handful of dates, but they didn't end on the best terms.

Fallon didn't think she'd see him again, let alone have him as a client, and now they're living under the same roof. Sounds like a recipe for disaster.

My phone buzzes with another text.

Fallon: Forgot to ask earlier. How's the wedding planning going?

Lila: It's going to come down to the wire, but it'll be perfect—it has to be!

Fallon: How are you holding up?

Lila: I'm so happy for Andrew and Hannah.

Fallon: You know that's not what I'm referring to.

Sometimes I think she knows me better than I do.

Lila: I'm okay, I promise!

Fallon: Someday, it'll be your turn. Just you wait and see!

Lila: What about you? I hate the idea of you spending Christmas alone.

Fallon: I'll manage. I've got an entire hockey stick collection here and two weeks to figure out the best ways to use them to get a rise out of Harrison.

Lila: Remind me to never get on your bad side.

Fallon: You could never.

Lila: I better get ready. It's going to be a long day. Good luck with the demon cat!

Fallon: I wonder if holy water would work...Kick ass today!

I slip out of bed, careful not to wake Winston, who is sprawled out at my feet, snoring loudly.

Despite having a perfectly acceptable dog bed, he insists on sleeping in mine. I'm powerless against his irresistible puppy dog eyes. Unlike most dogs, he takes his beauty sleep seriously and pouts for hours if I wake him up too early. Luckily, he's oblivious to my alarm clock, or we might have a problem.

After I grab the clothes that I laid out last night, I pad to the bathroom to get ready.

My one-bedroom cottage has an open floor plan, with

exposed wooden beams running across the ceiling, adding a rustic touch. There's a queen-sized bed in the corner, a reading nook by the window, and a kitchenette outfitted with stone countertops and copper accents. Off the main room is the bathroom with a walk-in shower, a free-standing tub and a skylight, allowing the natural light to filter in.

When Kay first suggested I stay here, I tried convincing her to let Winston and I have the innkeeper's room in the main building and have her move in here. However, she was insistent that Winston and I needed more space and privacy than she did. And she didn't want me to take on the added responsibility of being available to guests around the clock. Despite my assurance that I was happy to do it, she refused. Kay is the most stubborn person I know, and once she's made up her mind, there's no convincing her otherwise.

When I'm finished in the bathroom, I come out, take a seat on the bench by the front door, and put my boots on.

Winston's ears twitch, and he pries open one eye. As soon as he realizes I'm getting ready to leave, he springs up, races down his ramp at the foot of the bed, and barrels toward me with a chorus of excited yips.

"Good morning, Winn." I lean down to give him a good scratch behind the ear. "Looks like someone woke up in a good mood today." I pick a sweater from his winter collection that I keep in a nearby basket. This one is cream with a candy cane pattern and holly leaves woven into the design. "Let's get you dressed so we can head over to the inn."

He presses his paw against my leg, tail wagging in agreement. He lets me help him into his sweater, but as soon as I finish, he stands on his hind legs, pawing at the air, begging for a treat.

"It's impossible to resist when you're so darn cute." I grab a biscuit from the stash that I keep in the kitchenette and give it to him. "This is the only one you're getting from me today," I warn him as he greedily gobbles it up.

I have a feeling, between my mom and Kay, he's going to be extra spoiled this week.

After locking up the cottage and stopping in the yard so Winston can do his business, we head to the inn.

This early in the morning, the inn is peaceful, and the lobby is void of guests. There's already a fire in the stone fireplace, casting a warm glow on the beams overhead. Kay is an early bird, but after she makes her rounds, she usually goes back to her room to read before setting out fresh fruit and pastries for the guests. On the rare occasion I make it to the kitchen before her, I brew the first pot of coffee so she can have a fresh cup to start her day off right.

I stop short when I enter the kitchen. Brooks is standing at the workbench, locked in a fierce stare-down with a blender full of spinach, fruit, and protein powder. Judging by his scowl, the blender is winning their standoff.

He hasn't noticed me yet, but I can't seem to stop staring. He's ridiculously attractive in his gray sweatpants that sit low on his hips.

Oh my god.

I wasn't anticipating having a front-row seat to his bare chest, glistening with sweat, each flex of muscle emphasizing his six-pack.

He must've just come from the gym, and since Kay keeps the heat cranked up, he probably ditched his shirt to cool off.

I swallow hard. I've never had this kind of visceral reaction to a man. But it shouldn't surprise me that Brooks has the power to send my pulse to race and my mind wandering down a path it really shouldn't.

"Enjoying the view?" he asks.

My cheeks heat, and I avert my eyes from his chest. "What? No." I step over to the window by the sink and open it.

"It's forty-five degrees outside," Brooks deadpans.

I slam the window shut. "I figured you were hot."

"You think I'm hot?"

"Yes. I mean no. I mean…"

"You all right, Lila? You look a little flushed," he says with a smirk.

I clear my throat, square my shoulders, and point to the kitchen appliance. "I was just wondering what kind of battle plan you have for the blender. From here it looks like it has the upper hand."

Brooks shakes the blender in frustration "It's not my fault there's something wrong with it." His smirk drops to a scowl.

"Someone woke up on the wrong side of the bed," I tease.

"That would have been ideal." He grunts. "The inn is fully booked, so I had the pleasure of sleeping on a cot last night in the storage room. Not exactly five-star accommodations," he says, massaging the back of his neck.

"That explains your cheery mood this morning," I say with a playful smile.

I admit sleeping in the storage room sounds miserable. The inn does have fold-out beds we keep on hand, but they aren't all that comfortable.

I'm about to suggest he stay in my cottage, but stop short, remembering there's only one bed. Sure, he could bring his cot, but I don't think a change in location would be much of an upgrade.

With only three days left to plan this wedding, the last thing I need is Brooks walking around my place without a shirt, distracting me.

He repeatedly jabs the pulse button on the blender, his scowl deepening. "This thing is definitely busted."

I rest against the counter, covering my mouth to hide my grin.

"What's so funny?" he demands.

"Have you tried plugging it in?" I ask, nodding toward the base.

He scoffs. "Of course, the thing is—" His eyes follow my hand holding out the unplugged cord.

I lean over him to plug in the blender, the motor humming to life as the blades whirl until the mixture is perfectly smooth.

The sound drowns out the traitorous thump of my heart and the sharp gasp I take when my hip brushes against Brooks' thigh. His jaw is tight, and his eyes are narrowed like he's caught in a silent war with himself.

He finally turns the blender off, but his gaze remains on me. "You smell like peppermint and lavender," he says softly.

My knuckles turn white as I grip the counter. "It's my body wash," I whisper.

"It suits you." His voice is low.

Our faces are only inches apart, and I force myself to remain still, my body coming alive with him so close. My pulse is pounding in my ears as he traces my jawline with his thumb. Though it seems like an innocent gesture, the undercurrent of desire in his lingering touch sends my heart racing.

I'm unable to concentrate, my gaze trailing down his chest, along his abs, and to his V-line. He's devastatingly handsome, and I'm drunk off the exhilaration of being so close. When I glance up, his intense gaze is locked on mine. His eyes have a glimmer of fascination, and it could be my imagination, but I swear he leans in a fraction, almost inviting me to reciprocate his touch.

I'm instantly reminded of our kiss in the photo booth.

Brooks' hand gently cups my cheek as he traces the outline of my lips with his tongue. His eyes are dark and intense when I put my hands on his thighs, his breathing growing heavy under my touch.

I should have told him who I was before I let it get that far, but when he pulled me into his lap, I was lost in the heat of the moment, unable to think of anything but him.

The sound of Winston barking causes Brooks to withdraw in the present, and he glares down at my dog, who dared to interrupt.

Brooks is a contradiction—one minute, he's irritated with me, and the next he looks at me like I'm the only person around who matters. Not even the strongest barriers could shield me against his unpolished charm, and I'd be wise to keep my guard up when my heart is on the line.

I shift my attention to Winston, who's flopped on the floor, whining as if he's endured a lifetime of hunger.

I roll my eyes, laughing at his theatrics. "Honestly, Winn. You'd think I never feed you."

When I step away from the counter, Brooks gently grabs my wrist.

His eyes dart to my mouth before meeting my eyes. "Thanks for your help with the blender," he says softly.

I swallow hard. "Anytime." Here's to hoping my voice doesn't betray the fluttering in my chest.

"You better feed your dog," he adds, the ghost of a smile softening his usually serious features. "He's staring at me like he's plotting my demise for delaying his breakfast."

"Yeah, I should feed him before he gets any ideas," I tease.

As I walk toward the pantry with Winston in tow, I rub my wrist, unable to shake the longing for a few more seconds lost in the heat of Brooks' gaze.

It's barely noon, and today has already been a disaster. Half the glassware I ordered from the city arrived shattered, and finding tablecloths in the new color scheme is proving to be a challenge. The original colors were red, green, and gold, and despite Hannah's attempts to convince me otherwise, it was easy to tell that she didn't like them. Thanks to her Pinterest board, I know that she prefers blue and silver.

I'll do whatever it takes to make her vision come to life, even if it means sleepless nights and a hundred more calls until I find a vendor that has table clothes in the right color who can deliver before Christmas.

Now I'm staring at a small Christmas tree that was just delivered from Fir & Flurries, the local tree farm. The branches are mostly bare, with just a few stubborn needles hanging on, looking more like a coat rack than a holiday centerpiece. Whoever dropped it off didn't wait around for a signature, probably wanting to avoid my inevitable less-than-enthusiastic feedback.

"What the hell is that?" Brooks asks, stepping into the lobby.

After our encounter in the kitchen, he excused himself to Kay's office to take a few work calls. It reminds me that we couldn't be more different if we tried—he's the CEO of a renowned film production studio, living in a penthouse, and rubs shoulders with celebrities, while I'm just a small-town wedding planner who spends my Friday nights in bed with pizza, cookie dough ice cream, and my dog, binge-watching Hallmark movies. I particularly love the holiday ones, fantasizing about a whirlwind romance with a handsome stranger, snuggling by the fire, and having a spontaneous moment under the mistletoe.

"It's a tree," I reply, stating the obvious. "Andrew and Hannah carved their initials into a pine tree during one of their first dates, so I thought it would be a nice touch. The plan was to create ornament place settings to hang from the branches…" I trail off when I look at the sparsely needled limbs, debating if I should abandon the idea entirely.

Brooks scoffs. "That *thing* isn't a tree. It's a giant twig that's lost its dignity. What happened to the needles?"

I shrug. "Honestly, I'm not sure. It was just sitting outside like this with a Fir & Flurries tag attached to the top branch. Doug, who runs the tree farm, usually handles deliveries himself, but he must have gotten extra help this season."

"This is unacceptable," Brooks mutters.

He strides over to the reception desk, where Kay is supposedly busy reviewing inventory on the computer, although her attempt at eavesdropping is far from subtle.

"Can I borrow your truck?" Brooks asks her.

"Sure thing." She retrieves the keys from under the desk and hands them over. "Make sure you tell Doug I'm not ordering my Christmas tree from him next year if he doesn't fix this."

"My pleasure," Brooks calls over his shoulder.

I give him a puzzled look as he passes by. "Wait, where are you going?"

"*We're* going to the tree farm so you can pick out something that isn't one gust of wind away from snapping in half," he says, heading for the exit.

My mouth falls open as he strides toward the lobby entrance. He pauses just long enough to turn back, a frown crossing his face when he sees I'm not following him. "You coming or what?"

"Who else is going to make sure you pick a good one?" I quip.

He swings open the front door, and out of nowhere, Winston zips past him, assuming the invitation to go outside is meant for him. He barks enthusiastically, spinning in circles, urging me to follow.

"Have fun," Kay hollers from the front desk.

"We'll be back soon," I promise.

"Take your time. I'll hold down the fort while you're gone."

Brooks sighs, glancing out at Winston. "Guess this means the dog is coming?"

"His name is Winston, remember?" I remind him with a cheeky grin. "And yes, he is. Unless you want to be the one to tell him he has to stay behind." I motion to my dog, who is now bouncing around in a nearby snowbank, hopping like a rabbit. "Although, good luck trying to explain that to him when he's being this adorable—especially if he gives you his signature puppy dog eyes," I warn Brooks with a pat on the shoulder. "Don't worry. It won't be long before you accept that he calls the shots around here. It's Winn's world, and we're all lucky enough to live in it."

"Super," Brooks says, unamused. "Guess I'm swapping out entitled celebrities for a dog with attitude. Just my luck."

"At least Winston's loyalty doesn't come with a price tag," I counter. "Unless you factor in his treats and toy collection."

When we reach Kay's truck, I'm caught off guard when Brooks moves ahead of me to open the passenger door and offers me a hand as I climb in.

My breath catches at the contact. His hand is warm against mine and lingers just a moment longer than necessary. It's ridiculous how a small gesture can leave me feeling off balance, but there's something about the way my hand feels wrapped in his that makes my heart race.

I'm puzzled when he closes my door, worried he's reconsidered bringing Winston along. But a few seconds later, he climbs into the driver's seat, cradling my dog in his arms, and gently sets him on the seat between us.

Butterflies flutter in my stomach, and the romantic in me can't help but interpret the gesture as a sign that he cares, despite him acting aloof. I'm quick to remind myself that he's helping me as a favor to Andrew and doesn't share my sentiment. This isn't the plot of a romantic comedy unfolding.

"Thank you," I murmur, hoping he doesn't notice my voice wavering.

Winston climbs into my lap, adjusting his position so he can peer out the window. His ears perk up as we pull out of the parking lot and onto the road leading toward town.

When we get to Fir & Flurries, the parking lot is empty except for a work truck displaying their logo on the side.

As soon as we park, Doug, the owner, rushes over to greet us. He opens my door and gives me a side hug. "Lila, darling, what a pleasure. I didn't know if I'd get the chance to see you with all the events you've had at the inn lately."

From my peripheral vision, I see Brooks in his seat, a flicker of something unreadable flashing in his unwavering gaze.

"It's good to see you, Doug. I'm doing well; thanks for asking."

He helps me out of the truck, and the second I set Winston down, he wastes no time running to play in a nearby pile of snow.

"What can I do for you?" Doug asks.

A car door slams, followed by Brooks marching over, hands tucked in his pockets.

He comes to stand next to me, facing Doug. "You sent a tree to Whispering Pines that was missing its needles." His voice drips with annoyance. "It's better suited as firewood than decor for a wedding."

Doug visibly blanches, the color drawing from his face. "I'm sorry to hear that. We've been so busy that I hired someone from the local high school to deliver trees this weekend, and he must not have been paying attention when unloading the truck," Doug explains. "I'll personally hand-deliver a new one tonight."

Brooks shakes his head. "It's fine. We're here, so we might as well pick it out."

I rest my hand on his chest, silently urging him to dial it down a notch. Despite his surly attitude, I find it surprisingly sweet that he's looking out for me. Apart from my family, I'm not used to someone advocating for me like this.

Still, in a small town like Starlight Pines, a bit of compassion goes a long way. The last thing I want is to upset Doug and risk him sharing our unpleasant exchange with the other locals. As an event planner, there's no telling when I'll need to call in a favor, and I can't afford to burn bridges over one scraggly tree.

"What Brooks is trying to say is that we know you're busy, and we're more than happy to pick one out ourselves," I say, offering Doug a friendly smile.

He nods. "Certainly. Pick any tree you'd like." He gestures toward the rows of fir trees on the lot. "And Lila," he adds, his tone earnest, "Please convey my apologies to Kay. She's a long-standing customer, and I'll personally oversee future deliveries to the inn to make sure this doesn't happen again."

I lean forward to give his arm a reassuring squeeze. "We really appreciate it, Doug."

Just then, an SUV pulls into the parking lot and Willis and Leola Carter, the elderly couple who own the coffee shop in town, get out and head toward the tree lot.

"I'm going to help the Carters' now, but if you need anything, just holler," Doug says before jogging toward them.

"You're aware that being nice when someone messes up is an invitation to walk all over you, right?" Brooks informs me once Doug is out of earshot.

"Your grandma always says kindness opens doors that force can't. I've found from experience that people are much more likely to go the extra mile when I show them a little grace. Looks like you forgot the small-town way of doing things," I say, giving him a light tap on the shoulder.

We continue down the dirt path toward the tree lot. Winston leads the way, proudly carrying a giant stick in his mouth, dragging it on the ground as he trots forward, uncaring that it's bigger than he is.

"That's a nice sentiment, but in the real world, people see kindness as a sign of weakness," Brooks says.

I stop mid-stride and put a hand on my hip. "Are you calling me weak?"

"I'm saying you could easily get taken advantage of. Hence the reason we're here. Doug sent you a half-assed tree."

I rise on my tiptoes and poke my finger against his chest. "In case you haven't noticed, Starlight Pines isn't the cutthroat corporate jungle you're used to. Here, folks are more interested in supporting each other than playing the blame game." I turn on my heel, then whirl back around to face Brooks and add, "And for the record, I'm far from weak. I'm considerate, upbeat, and always give people the benefit of the doubt. I believe in second chances, which in my opinion makes me strong and reliable. And…why are you looking at me like that?"

Brooks is gazing down at me, his expression mixed with amusement and a faint smirk.

He lifts a finger to move a stray piece of hair behind my ear. "You're cute when you're angry."

I'm taken aback by his comment.

"Cute? I prefer stunning and witty," I say, half-kidding. "Now let's go find that tree, shall we?" I add, turning away to hide the slight brush creeping up my neck. "Lead the way," Brooks says, motioning for me to take the lead down the winding path.

Once we get to the tree lot, we navigate through the never-ending rows, with Winston bounding ahead. He's abandoned the giant stick and has his nose to the ground, inspecting each tree, occasionally kicking up snow in his search for the perfect scent.

Brooks walks by my side with his hands shoved in his pockets. "Does your dog always wear sweaters?" He nods toward Winston, who's leaving a trail of paw prints behind. "He has a new one on every time I see him."

"In the winter he does. When I adopted him from the animal shelter, he was a scrawny little thing and couldn't stop shaking like a leaf. My mom knitted him a sweater so he wouldn't be cold, and now she's practically his personal tailor."

The pet adoption coordinator told me that Winston was the runt of his litter and the last to be adopted. That's partly why I instantly fell in love with him. I can relate to feeling like you've been left behind and not knowing what the future holds.

Winston deserved to be adopted by someone who would give him a chance to thrive and shower him with the love and attention he deserves.

Three years later, he's surrounded by people who treat him like the special dog he is and spoil him to no end.

"You're still close with your parents, huh?" Brooks asks.

"Yeah. We've always been tight-knit," I say, kicking a pinecone across the dirt. "When Andrew moved away after he graduated high school, it was just the three of us left at home until I went to live at the cottage. Even now, Winston and I spend every Sunday at their place, and my mom pops by the inn often to help Kay out, especially when it gets busy or if I'm running an event."

Brooks rubs the back of his neck, a faint crease forming between his brows. "My grandma is lucky to have you. She told me that you've been driving her to all her doctor's appointments and managing things at the inn when it gets to be too much for her. You must think my brothers and I are bad people for not stepping up sooner."

Kay never explained why they don't visit, but I assume it has something to do with their dad passing away. Every year on the anniversary of his death, Kay retreats to her room. Losing her only child must have been unimaginable, and there was nothing I could do to take away the pain.

Each spring, we plant a fir tree in his memory, and once they're all full-grown, we'll decorate each one with Christmas lights during the holidays.

"Of course not," I say gently. "Is there a particular reason you and your brothers stayed away for so long?"

Brooks looks down at his boots, kicking up pieces of dirt and snow as we walk. "I can't speak for my brothers, but for me, life got in the way. Work mainly."

I scoff. "You can't possibly work *all* the time."

"More or less. When I started my own production company, I threw everything I had into it. If I hadn't put in the effort, someone else would have, and I wouldn't be the one with a studio that pulls in record-breaking profits."

"Kay is really proud of you. She's always glowing after a summer visit to one of your movie sets. Although, she's a tad disappointed that she still hasn't met her favorite actor from *Wicked.*

"She's the only person who can make A-listers feel like they're auditioning for *her* approval."

"Has filmmaking always been your passion?"

Brooks gives me a wistful smile, sliding his hands into his pocket. "Yeah. It was how my dad and I bonded after my mom left. He was obsessed with action movies, and every Friday night, we'd watch one together. He used to joke that in another life he would have been a film producer, but being a lawyer was the more practical choice."

Hearing more about his past makes me think Brooks' abrasive behavior is a way of coping with the grief, using it as a way to shield himself from the pain of losing someone he loved. He may not want my sympathy, but that doesn't stop me from wanting to find a way to show him that he doesn't have to face everything alone.

I rest my hand on his arm. "Your grandma understands why being here is hard, and she doesn't blame you for staying away. What matters is that you're here now."

He visibly relaxes, and I find it difficult to breathe when he moves closer. His brooding demeanor drops momentarily, and I'm drawn to this glimpse of his gentler side, usually reserved for his grandma.

An expression I can't decipher flickers across his features, and my heart rate speeds up when his gaze flits across my face, lingering on the spot just above my mouth.

"Is something wrong?" I whisper.

"You have a snowflake on your face," he says softly.

My breath hitches when he reaches out and drags his thumb across my chin; grazing my lower lip, his fingers resting lightly on my jaw. A spark of electricity ripples through me at the unexpected warmth of his hand, making me glad he's not wearing gloves. I'm frozen in place, unable to control my body's reaction. The intensity in his eyes mirrors how I feel.

It would be so easy to fall for Brooks, fueled by a teenage crush I wish I could leave behind. Yet, each time we touch, a familiar spark ignites, giving me a glimmer of hope that this isn't just a figment of my imagination—that he might feel it too.

The sound of footsteps crunching over the snow has Brooks snapping out of it first, blinking rapidly and shaking his head. He jerks his arm back to his side, flexing his hand.

"There I go touching you again," he mutters to himself. "It's a challenge where you're concerned."

"Was there even a snowflake?" I tease, giving him a tentative smile, and attempting to keep my voice steady.

He dips his chin with a groan and avoids my gaze. "We should pick a tree so we can get back to the inn. Your family will be there soon, and we don't want to keep them waiting."

"Yeah," I say, dipping my head.

When we round the corner, Winston is next to a balsam fir with evenly spaced branches, each one full of dark green needles. I can already picture how it'll look with white lights twinkling through the branches, draped with white ribbon and silver ornaments. This tree will be the perfect addition to the wedding decor.

"This is the one," I announce.

"Great," Brooks says, rolling up his sleeves. "I'll load it onto the truck bed."

"Thank you," I say with a broad smile. "I couldn't have done this without you."

He opens his mouth like he wants to speak but doesn't say anything. After a few seconds, he nods curtly before turning around to lift the tree and carry it in the direction of the truck. I'm left in the quiet tree lot, wondering why it feels like he's purposely avoiding getting close to me.

CHAPTER 4

Brooks

"Brooks, dear, can you get me a couple of bottles of wine?" Grandma asks while assembling a Caesar salad.

"Sure thing." I head to the pantry and grab two bottles from the wine fridge. Once back in the kitchen, I hold them up for her approval. "Merlot work?"

"That's perfect."

"Need anything else?"

"That should be it." She drizzles a generous amount of dressing over the salad, adds a sprinkle of parmesan, and tosses it before stepping back to admire her work. "How'd you sleep last night?" she asks.

"Do you actually let guests sleep on that cot?" I ask, rubbing the back of my neck. "The frame sags and it creaks with every move."

She gives me a quick wave of her hand. "It's better than the floor, isn't it?"

"That's debatable," I mutter.

At six-two, even a decent cot would be cramped, but a nearly broken one becomes a torture contraption designed to keep me awake and sore all night.

"Do you have another cot I could swap it out with?"

"Why don't you take the Merlot and the Ceaser salad into the dining room?" Grandma says, holding out the bowl. "Lila will help me bring out the rest of the food after she's finished taking Winston outside."

"Uh, yeah, sure." I wonder why she ignored my question about my sleeping arrangements but I decide to ask her about it later.

A few minutes later, we're all gathered around the large farmhouse table, including the Monroe family, their friends from town, and me and Grandma. She carries out a steaming pot of her famous beef stew, the rich aroma filling the room. I can't recall the last time I sat down for a home-cooked meal. Typically, I'm busy wining and dining clients and talent at upscale restaurants, and on the rare evenings I'm home, I microwave one of the meals my housekeeper has prepared for me.

The inn doesn't provide full-service meals for guests since Grandma never wanted the hassle of a kitchen staff. She prefers to support the local restaurants instead. Still, she loves cooking for guests and family on special occasions and insisted that Lila include dinner at Whispering Pines in the wedding week itinerary.

Lila follows behind with two large baskets of sourdough bread, setting them on either end of the table. She's changed into a red knee-length dress with bell sleeves and a pair of silver flats. Her long, golden tresses are pulled back into a half ponytail with a bright red bow that matches her dress.

"Thank you, dear," Grandma says, patting Lila on the shoulder as she walks past.

"Of course," Lila replies.

"You've outdone yourself, Kay. Everything smells delicious," Andrew says with a grin.

"Yes, thanks so much for doing this," Hannah chimes in.

"Absolutely. You're all busy with wedding prep, so it's the

least I could do. I'm so happy that you're celebrating your special day here and on Christmas no less."

She gives her head a small shake when Lila reaches for the chair next to her. "You're next to Brooks tonight." She motions to where I'm seated a couple of chairs down.

"Oh." Lila whips her head around to face me, her eyes wide with surprise. "I didn't realize we had assigned seating,"

"Tonight we do," Grandma says.

Lila comes around the table, and as she moves to sit, I instinctively stand up and pull out her chair, catching Andrew's sharp stare from across the table. Can't say I blame him. No one's ever accused me of being a gentleman. Don't get me wrong—I'm not a complete asshole. I'll treat a woman to an expensive dinner before taking her to bed, but going around acting like Prince Charming? That's not me.

Yet, I'm quickly learning that Lila isn't just another woman to impress. Her presence dulls the chaotic energy thrumming through me, making me feel strangely more at peace than I have in a while. She lights up the room when she walks in, her laughter like a breath of fresh air, which has me doing more than I normally would for a woman to make her feel special.

She bats her eyelashes as she slides in. "Are you going to get my napkin, too?"

"Didn't realize I'd signed up to be your assistant," I grumble in a forced show of annoyance as I reach across to grab her napkin off the table and place it gently on her lap.

Andrew is still watching us with a furrowed brow so I clear my throat and take my seat.

With practiced hands, Grandma dishes up bowls of beef stew, handing them out one by one around the table before we all start to dig in.

"The tree you and Brooks picked out earlier today is stunning," Grandma remarks to Lila, her face glowing with approval.

"Yes. It's perfect," Hannah adds from her spot across the table. "Making ornament place settings for the wedding was a genius idea. You're brilliant, Lila."

She blushes as she takes a sip of wine. "Thanks; I'm glad you like it."

Andrew leans forward, his hands clasped. "Working hard to secure 'favorite sibling' status, huh, sis?"

Lila snorts, shooting him a playful glare. "I'm your *only* sibling, smartass."

"Watch your language, please," Grandma chides, raising a finger in warning.

"Says the person who cussed old man Barker out last week," Lila quips.

"That's because he forgot the box of walnuts with my order. When I pointed it out, he suggested I go to the store myself. I told him I knew exactly where to find big ones that would be far more satisfying than anything he could offer."

I almost choke on my drink, stunned by my grandma's crassness. Meanwhile, everyone else at the table bursts into laughter, unable to contain their amusement.

Lila leans back in her chair, a napkin covering her mouth as she giggles uncontrollably. "I can't get over what you said. Mr. Barker hasn't been able to look you in the eye since."

Observing their interaction makes me realize just how special the relationship between Grandma and Lila is. Grandma treats her with the affection and care she would a granddaughter, and while my brothers and I have been absent, I'm grateful she's had someone she could depend on in our place.

"Still," Grandma says, pointing at Lila. "Do as I say, not as I do."

"Sorry, Kay," Lila ducks her head, her tone apologetic.

I lean in and whisper in her ear. "Don't worry, she's called me out for my foul language, too."

Lila laughs quietly. "Is swearing your *thing*?"

"Just a bad habit I've never broken. What's your excuse?"

"I grew up with an older brother," she retorts.

"Hey, I heard that," Andrew protests, though his grin is unmistakable.

"Behave, you two," their mom interjects.

"Yes, Mom," they say in unison.

Everyone goes back to eating their beef stew and bread. The rest of dinner with the Monroes and Grandma feels like old times. It's a loud, chaotic, and lively affair. Andrew and Lila might be eight years apart, but they tease each other mercilessly, and the love they share is unmistakable. It makes me miss my own brothers, wishing they were here to celebrate with us.

After dinner, we move into the lounge area near the lobby for a nightcap. Lila's mom made a batch of Irish coffee and shortbread cookies. The lights are dimmed, and Christmas music is playing in the background while everyone mingles.

Andrew and Hannah are snuggled in an armchair near the crackling fire. Hannah is nestled in Andrew's lap, her head resting on his shoulder, and his arm is wrapped around his waist. He plays idly with her hair, winding a strand around his finger while she talks. They've never been afraid to show affection in public, and at first, it caught me off guard. I couldn't understand how Andrew could so freely let someone in and trust her not to break his heart.

On paper, that kind of connection sounds like everything I should want, but my distorted perspective prevents me from believing that love is anything but complicated. It's messy, demands a level of trust I'm unsure I can give, and requires a balancing act of expectations that often result in disappointment.

The only example of a relationship I had as a kid was a

dysfunctional one. My mom walked out on my dad when my brothers and I were kids, and the few memories I have of my parents together are chaotic, marked by heated arguments and slammed doors. I couldn't understand how she could leave if she loved us. The experience left me jaded and questioning the emotion altogether.

Andrew and Hannah are the exception. They've faced challenges most couples couldn't survive, yet somehow, they've weathered the storm, demonstrating that true love does exist for some. I'm too cynical, too guarded to let anyone that close. Still, watching them, I can't help but wonder what it might be like to find someone who's worth the risk.

I don't realize I'm scowling until Andrew glances over, arching a brow as if to question why I'm in a bad mood. Wanting to steer clear of an invitation to talk with him and Hannah, I divert my gaze and move across the room, pretending that I'm looking for someone.

I'm seconds away from hiding out in the kitchen when I notice Lila near one of the floor-to-ceiling windows, holding her mug close to her chest as she looks outside at the snowy landscape. She has a white shawl wrapped around her shoulders that she wasn't wearing at dinner, framing the delicate curve of her collarbone.

Her blonde hair cascades down her back, and images of gripping it tightly as I lick a trail up her neck runs through my mind. I'd nuzzle my nose against her cheek, breathing in her sweet scent, stopping as I reach her lips, heightening the anticipation of where I would put my mouth next.

It might not be so tempting if I didn't already know what it felt like to have her within arm's reach. There's no denying she is gorgeous, and I've done everything in my power to keep my runaway thoughts at bay these past few months. Hell, it was easy when we on opposite sides of the country, yet now that we're in the same room, my dick is taking this moment to protest my decision to stay at arm's length.

I drag a hand over my face, determined to shake off this absurd liquor-induced fever dream. It must be the whiskey going to my head.

I'm puzzled when I look up just in time to catch sight of a flash of fur as Winston crashes into my legs, my drink sloshing from the glass, soaking the top half of my light gray pants. He stumbles back, dazed but otherwise oblivious of the mess he's created.

Lila gasps. "Oh, no," she exclaims as she rushes over. "Brooks, I'm so sorry. I kept Winn in your grandma's office during dinner and wanted to give him a chance to stretch his legs. He was so ready to be free and forgot to contain himself." She sets her own drink down on a nearby side table.

A few people glance in our direction but quickly return to their own conversations.

"I can help with that," she motions to the stain. "Follow me."

She tugs on my hand, and I don't bother resisting as she guides me over to the reception desk, where she grabs a bag full of hand items like breath mints, safety pins, and a mini first-aid kit. She rummages through it, pulling out a pack of wipes and takes a few out.

My breath hitches when she drops to her knees, and I have to look up at the ceiling and take a deep breath. Without a word, she pulls the fabric taut around my crotch, her fingers digging into the material as she rubs the stain vigorously. She furrows her brow in concentration as she scrubs harder, muttering to herself how spiked coffee is a pain in the ass to remove.

I breathe through my nose, trying to rein in my visceral reaction to the irresistible woman kneeling before me. Unfortunately, my dick didn't get the memo that Lila isn't there to pleasure me, and grows hard under her touch. I can tell the second she notices when her hand freezes above my zipper. Looking down, I see her mouth parting lightly, and her breaths are fast and shallow. Based on her reaction, I'd assume she likes what she sees, which makes me get harder.

Lila snaps her head up, her gaze locking onto mine. "Oh. Um…I'm sorry." She yanks her hand away and scrambles to stand up.

My instincts scream for me to reach and steady her, but I resist the impulse, forcing my hands to remain at my sides.

"Don't worry. It's just a stain," I say, knowing damn well that's not what she's referring to.

With a downcast gaze, she clutches her hands close to her chest. "Sorry the wipes didn't do the trick," she murmurs.

"You use that thing often?" I nod toward the bag on the counter.

She nods, tucking a stray hair behind her ear. "As a wedding planner, I have to be ready for anything. You'd be amazed by how messy cake cutting can get." She chuckles nervously. "Listen, this might sound like an odd request, but if you come back with me to my cottage, I have a stain remover pen that should work on that." She gestures toward the wet spot on my pants. "I used to have one in my bag, but I had to replace it and keep forgetting to bring the new one over."

I should say no.

I packed a similar pair of pants, and changing would only take a few minutes. In fact, it's getting late, and I should head to bed soon anyway. After staying up late last night making work calls and sleeping on a stiff, rickety cot that felt like it would give out at any second, the exhaustion is finally setting in.

Still, this could be my only chance to see the inside of Lila's cottage, and I'm genuinely curious about the personal touches she'd added to make it her own. I find myself willing to take any opportunity I can to learn more about her.

"I can go if we make it quick," I say.

"Yeah, okay," she agrees.

Thank god everyone else is too wrapped up in their own conversations to notice us slip out the back door. Winston has settled into a dog bed near the fireplace, seemingly happy to stay behind.

I follow closely behind Lila, down a pathway illuminated by string lights toward the cottage nestled in the trees. She swings open the gate of a white picket fence, leading us to the cottage with clapboard siding and a steep gabled roof. The windows are framed by black shutters, and flower boxes hang below, brimming with snow. A festive holiday wreath with red berries and pinecones hangs on the front door.

When we step inside, Lila's familiar scent floods my senses.

The space has been transformed since I last saw it. What was once just a functional space with the essentials, now feels like a home.

A small artificial Christmas tree is set up in the corner, draped with colorful lights, strings of popcorn, and woodland creature ornaments. There's a queen bed against the far wall with a gray comforter and an assortment of decorative pillows, and a small ramp is positioned at the foot of the bed.

That's when I notice the collection of snow globes lined up on the mantle above the small fireplace—each displaying a miniature scene of various snow-covered towns or bustling Christmas markets.

"Are these all from places that you've visited?"

A shadow briefly passes over Lila's expression. "I wish. Most were tokens of appreciation from brides who send them from their honeymoon destinations. But there are a handful that I've ordered online of places I'd like to visit someday."

She picks up a snow globe showcasing a small village market, each stall decorated with garland, and a towering Christmas tree in the middle. After giving it a shake, the glitter inside swirls around below, gently drifting down like snowfall as she sets it back on the mantle, letting out a soft sigh.

"Which of these places *have* you been to?" I motion to her collection.

She shakes her head, her lip caught between her teeth. "To be honest, my trip to California for Andrew and Hannah's engagement party is only one of the few times I've ventured outside of Vermont." She picks up another snow globe from Dublin with the original Saint Patrick's Cathedral in the center. "We didn't travel much growing up, and I started working with Kay right after high school. Wedding season runs year-round, so I haven't had much time for longer trips."

It's hard to ignore the nagging thought that I'm partly responsible for her staying put. Her sense of duty to my grandma keeps her rooted in Starlight Pines, and it pains me to know she hasn't had the chance to explore the places that decorate her shelf but not her memories.

"If you could travel anywhere in the world, where would it be?" I question.

She runs a hand over the glass of the snow globe still in her hand. "The question is where *wouldn't* I want to go? I want to watch the Northern Lights in Iceland, ice skate at Rockefeller Center, snorkel in the Great Barrier Reef, or even skinny dip on Red Beach in Santorini.

My brows shoot up. "Skinny dip?"

She looks at me with a playful grin, the corner of her eyes crinkling. "Why not? It sounds freeing, doesn't it? I've spent my entire life playing it safe, and sometimes I want to just throw caution to the wind and try something that gives me a rush."

I could think of several things that would give her a rush, and none of them require leaving this cottage.

Lila's attraction to me is palpable—the way her gaze wandered my body when we were in the kitchen this morning, and the way her tongue grazed her lip just now, her chest rising with each shallow breath.

I rest my hand over hers, carefully taking the snow globe and setting it back on the mantle. Her eyes meet mine, deep and seductive, and she lifts her chin, leaning in slightly so her breasts brush against my chest, making my mind go blank.

Fuck.

It requires every ounce of resistance I have not to grab her by the waist and kiss her again like I've wanted to since the first time in that cramped photo booth.

Lila's gaze shifts, and despite my internal protests, the tension between us fades when she steps back. "I should probably get that stain remover stick," she murmurs.

I nod. "Good idea," I concur, though my cock isn't in agreement.

She goes over to the kitchenette and rummages through a drawer before coming over with a stain remover pen in hand.

Lila stops short when she gets close to me, a blush spreading across her cheeks. "I should probably let you handle it from here." She holds out the spot remover.

"Thanks."

After twisting the cap off, I dab the stain on my pants.

Out of the corner of my eye, I catch Lila stealing a glance at me before she looks away. "You're welcome to stay here if you'd like," she offers, training her gaze on her collection of snow globes. "There's only one bed, but I tend to stay on my side, thanks to Winston. He's decided his own bed is inadequate"—she nods toward a fluffy dog bed in the corner—"and insists on sharing mine most nights."

I glance at the bed then back at her, battling the lure of giving in while logic tells me to stay away. Sleeping in tight quarters with the woman who's been occupying my thoughts would be playing with fire, and the desire to let it consume me might be impossible to resist.

My gaze lingers on her for a moment longer than it should. "Thanks for the offer, but I'll be fine in the storage room," I say, keeping my voice steady.

She shrugs. "Well, the offer stands if you change your mind." She scrunches her face, and I'm not sure if she's disappointed or just being polite.

It's time for me to go.

"You were right; this thing works wonders." I hand her the stain remover and take a step toward the door. "See you tomorrow, Lila."

Once I'm outside, I give myself a mental high-five. If self-control was an Olympic sport, I'd be taking home the gold medal tonight.

Given my recent track record where she's concerned, it's no less than a miracle that I kept my hands to myself. I know Lila is off-limits, yet, she's the whole damn package. She's gorgeous, compassionate, and generous, giving without expecting anything in return. Every small gesture has me inching closer to the edge slowly chipping away at my defenses.

CHAPTER 5

Lila

WHEN I RETURNED TO THE INN TO GET WINSTON, KAY and my parents were still in the lobby chatting with a group of guests who'd stopped by for refreshments. Andrew and Hannah had already gone back to my parents' house, likely taking advantage of having the place to themselves for a little while.

Brooks must have gone to bed after he left the cottage because he was nowhere to be found.

I'm still reeling from the fact that I practically felt him up in public—while on my knees, no less. That should have been the end of it, but naturally, I had to go and embarrass myself further by inviting him back to my place and offering for him to spend the night.

Way to go, Lila. You might as well have stripped naked, put a ribbon around yourself, and laid under a tree for him.

Winston and I are back at our cottage now. It's late, but instead of trying to get some sleep, I'm pacing the length of the entry rug, stopping at the edge before turning around and striding to the other end. Winston is sprawled on my bed, staring at me with judgment in his eyes.

I stop mid-stride with my hands on my hips. "You know, this is all your fault, right? If you hadn't run into Brooks, he wouldn't have spilled his drink, and I wouldn't have made a fool of myself."

He gives me a pointed look before flopping his head onto his paws, clearly over this conversation. "I'll remember that the next time you want a belly rub," I mutter. He doesn't so much as blink, knowing full well I'll cave when the time comes.

My one-sided debate is cut short by a knock at the door. No one ever comes to the cottage aside from Kay or my parents, and I already said goodnight to them before I left the inn.

I toss on a short silk robe, and when I crack the door open, I'm shocked to find Brooks on my porch, suitcase in hand and a backpack slung over his shoulder.

"Spill another drink?" I tease, arching a brow.

"Does your offer still stand for me to stay here tonight?" His tone is earnest.

I'm caught off guard by his request, looking back inside at my bed, which somehow seems far smaller than it is.

"Couldn't handle another night in the storage room after all?"

A frown crosses his face. "The damn cot collapsed as soon as I set my suitcase on it, not to mention it's freezing in there."

I cover my mouth, trying not to laugh. "Good thing you weren't in it. Small victories, right?" I say with a smile. "I'd hate to explain that trip to the ER."

The silence stretches on, and I wonder if he regrets his decision to come back. His gaze shifts lower, and my eyes follow to where my loosely tied robe has parted enough, revealing my dark green tank top and matching shorts.

Heat floods my cheeks as I tug the robe tighter, acutely aware of how exposed I am under his watch—yet there's a small part of me that doesn't want him to look away as his eyes trace every inch of my bare legs.

I steady my breathing to collect myself. "Why don't you come in?" I step aside to let him pass.

He snaps his head up, a flicker of heat flashing in his eyes before disappearing behind an unreadable calm.

"Thanks."

The door creaks as he steps inside, and I can't help but feel the weight of his presence.

My brain screams at me to play it cool, but I can't resist watching him from the corner of my eye as he sets his backpack and luggage against the wall and takes off his shoes.

My hands are clammy as I push a stray piece of hair behind my ear.

"You remember where the bathroom is?" I nod toward the connecting door.

Brooks glances over at me. "Yeah. I won't be long."

He collects a toiletry bag from his suitcase, offering me a quick nod before heading to the bathroom, shutting the door behind him.

I'm frozen in place, nibbling on my lower lip as I stare at the bathroom door, unsure what I've gotten myself into. I've just agreed to let my brother's best friend stay with me tonight. In *my* bed, no less. This is a recipe for disaster, inviting temptation that I've been doing my best to avoid since he arrived in Starlight Pines.

I distract myself by lifting Winston off my bed and setting him on the ground. He whines in protest, and I lean down to rub his head. "Sorry, buddy," I whisper. "You have to sleep in your own bed tonight. Mine is taken."

His tail flicks with irritation as he drags himself to his dog bed. After shifting from one side to the other in search of the perfect spot, he finally collapses onto the cushion with an exasperated sigh. He might be irritated with me tonight, but in the morning, he'll forget all about it when he wants his breakfast.

I toss the decorative pillows onto the armchair in the corner and pull back the comforter.

"What am I supposed to do now?" I ask Winston, earning a blank look that suggests I'm on my own.

The silence is heavy, pressing in on me. I consider texting Fallon, but she's most likely asleep.

Besides, there's nothing she could do except remind me I'm the one who invited Brooks to stay in the first place. Who am I kidding? She'd probably tell me I'm overthinking and that I should make a move on him while I had the opportunity.

I mull over the idea again of having Brooks sleep on the floor but quickly dismiss it. After a night on a cot in the storage room, and with no sleeping bag available, he'd have an even worse experience on the hardwood floor. The next couple of days are going to be busy with wedding preparations, and he's going to need to be well-rested.

I'm a brave, capable, and resilient woman. I can do hard things—including sharing a bed with my brother's attractive best friend, who I've hopelessly been pining for longer than I'd like to admit.

Thank god I took a shower and even shaved my legs before he showed up.

The reminder is both reassuring and disappointing. Come the day after Christmas, Brooks will go back to California, and I'll be alone in my cottage with my dog and my snow globes.

I'm startled by the sound of the bathroom door clicking open, causing me to take my robe off and toss it on top of the dresser before diving into bed. I quickly smooth out my hair and tugging the covers over my lap, trying to look casual.

Brooks steps into the room wearing nothing but a pair of black sweats. His feet are bare, and his back is on display, giving me a glimpse of his bare broad shoulders, as he bends slightly to plug his phone into the charger he brought with him by the kitchenette and reads something on the screen.

Unable to help myself, my gaze peruses the defined contours and dips of muscle that are like a work of art. When he turns in my direction, his eyes are still glued to whatever is on his phone, giving me a chance to gawk at his equally impressive washboard abs.

My mind wanders to what it might be like to run my fingers along every ridge as I trace down toward his happy trail, slowly moving lower and lower until my fingers curl around his shaft. I haven't seen him fully naked, but judging by the bulge in his pants, it's safe to say the man is well-endowed.

Heat rushes to my cheeks when he looks in my direction, and I avert my gaze to Winston just in time. Thank god I managed to snap out of my fantasy before he noticed me ogling him like a kid in a candy store. It's hardly my fault that he keeps walking around without a shirt on and looks like a model who's stepped off a magazine cover, practically begging for my attention.

After a few minutes, Brooks sets his phone on the counter and strides across the room. My eyes widen when he climbs into the bed next to me. "What are you doing?" I ask, my voice coming out breathless.

"Calling it a night," he states as he stretches out, looking entirely too comfortable. "Unless you've changed your mind about sharing the bed."

I snort. "You can't sleep here dressed like that." I motion toward his bare chest. "Don't you think you should put on a T-shirt when you're sharing a bed with a stranger?"

Not that I can say from experience, since I've never spent the night with someone I didn't know. And the few times I have had sex, I preferred to go home afterward. Not the most romantic option, but it keeps things uncomplicated and allows me to avoid the awkward morning-after conversation when I don't see the relationship going anywhere.

Brooks fluffs his pillow, casually brushing away a stray piece of dog hair. "We're not strangers." He settles on his side, facing me, his head resting on his hand. "We've known each other since we were kids."

Like I could forget.

"Doesn't mean you *know* me," I counter. "I bet you couldn't recall three things about my childhood."

"Challenge accepted." He chuckles, his eyes crinkling at the corners, a warmth there I haven't noticed before. "Your middle name is Sage, after your maternal grandmother. When you were eight, you set up a shop in your living room with items you *borrowed* from Andrew and me, including my favorite video game and one of his textbooks. You insisted that we pay you if we wanted our stuff back. I admit, it was a brilliant operation."

My stomach flips as a rush of warmth flows through me. They might be small details, but the fact that he paid attention, even back when I was his best friend's annoying kid sister, means something.

I straighten my spine. "That's only two things."

"You were always smiling. Whenever I'd come over to hang out with Andrew, you'd greet me at the door with a new joke from a Laffy Taffy wrapper. Even when we got annoyed that you'd follow us around, you were unfazed." He leans in closer, the heat of his skin burning a hole through my T-shirt, making the space between us feel impossibly small. "I even taught you to ride a bike, or did you forget about that?"

How could I ever forget?

"I remember," I whisper.

The year Andrew and Brooks moved to California, they both came back to Starlight Pines for the holidays. They surprised me with a bike for Christmas, and I sheepishly admitted that I'd never learned to ride. After one too many falls during my dad's attempts to teach me when I was younger, I had sworn off biking for good.

Brooks was horrified and insisted they cancel the double date they had planned that afternoon with some girls they had went to high school with so he could teach me. At first, Andrew complained about their change in plans, but he went along with it because Brooks wouldn't take no for an answer.

"If you still think I don't know you, I can even list three things I've noticed about you since I got here." His steady voice breaks through the silence. "You prefer a mocha instead of regular coffee. When you're nervous, you chew on your lower lip, and I'm pretty sure your obsession with Christmas is borderline unhealthy." His voice turns playful at the end.

The butterflies in my stomach are in overdrive as I gaze at the man who was once my idol, now the object of my most vivid fantasies. My heart may be able to steady itself, but I can't stop staring at his corded arms and the way his eyes are trained on mine, as if starved for something more.

Before I do something reckless, like throw myself at him, I reach over to turn off the bedside lamp. It may be dark, but there's a faint light from the moon casting a soft glow in the room. In the silence, all I can hear is our breathing and my erratic heart that's beating like a drum.

"Want to hear something funny?" I whisper into the stillness. "When I was younger, I had a crush on you. It sounds silly, but you always let me tag along with you and Andrew, making me feel special whenever you were around." I hesitate, heart pounding. "Honestly, I'm not sure if those feelings ever went away." I press my lips together, mortified by my own confession. With the lights off, it felt like I could be brave, even if for just a moment.

Just when I think he's not going to respond, he breaks the silence. "I haven't stopped thinking about you since the night of Andrew and Hannah's engagement party. The second you smiled at me, I knew things were different, and after our kiss, I knew I was done for."

His confession sends a shiver down my spine and is something I only ever dreamed of. Hearing him admit that he thinks about me sends a prickling heat rising to my chest and spreading through my veins like a slow-burning flame.

Brooks' hand finds mine in the darkness, squeezing gently before pulling away, leaving me craving more of his touch.

"Good night, Goldie."

I swallow hard, stunned at the sound of the nickname he used to call me as a kid. I always liked it, but hearing him use it now leaves me momentarily breathless.

Brooks turns on his side, facing the wall, his back grazing mine, but he doesn't move away. I remain still, concentrating on controlling my breathing. I press my thighs together, determined to banish the impulse to turn around and wrap my arm around him from behind. But it's difficult when the man of my dreams is in my bed and he just confessed I've been on his mind as much as he's been on mine.

As I lie there, hoping sleep will come, I think back to when he taught me how to ride a bike. It was the day my crush began—a twelve-year-old's innocent infatuation with her brother's best friend.

"Alright, Lila, sit up straight with your eyes forward," Brooks instructs once I'm seated on the bike.

"What if I fall again?"

"Then I'll catch you," he says. "I promise," he adds, his tone warm when he notices I'm shaking like a leaf.

I tuck my lip between my teeth, trying to steady my nerves. "I'm really not sure I can do this. Can we try another time?" I suggest.

Brooks shakes his head. "Riding a bike is a rite of passage, and you've already waited long enough to learn." He carefully puts a helmet on my head and gives it a light tap for good measure. "It's going to be okay."

Andrew glances up from his phone and gives me a thumbs up.

"You've got this, Lila," he says, shooting me an encouraging smile. "I'll be here cheering you on."

"Thanks, Andrew," I say with a grin. "Okay, I think I'm ready," I tell Brooks.

"I want you to start pedaling as soon as I give you a little push," he instructs.

I take a deep breath and push down on the pedals, gripping the handlebars like my life depends on them—because it feels like it does. The bike begins to wobble, and just when I think I'm going to fall, Brooks steadies me.

"You've got this," he repeats, his hand holding the back of the seat to keep me steady.

I focus on the driveway ahead, my legs pumping with renewed energy as Brooks matches my pace, his encouragement fueling my determination.

"Just like that," he cheers. "You're doing it, Goldie."

I beam at hearing his nickname for me. He says it's because of my sunny disposition.

I glance over to see him grinning. It's one of the few times I've seen him genuinely happy. He's usually so serious, but right now, that smile causes a flutter in my chest, and I question if my feelings for him are more than just admiration.

Before I risk losing my balance, I focus my attention forward, laughing as the wind nips at my cheeks. The crunch of snow under my tires is proof that I'm actually riding a bike, sending a rush of excitement through me.

I'm brought back to the present when Brooks shifts beside me, a reminder that my childhood crush has evolved into a tangible desire to be his.

"Good night, Brooks," I whisper into the dark.

CHAPTER 6

Brooks

A S I SHIFT IN BED, I'M AWARE OF LILA DRAPED ACROSS MY chest. Her head is nestled in the crook of my shoulder, with one leg hitched over my thigh and an arm wrapped securely around my waist. Blonde tresses fan out across her pillow, and her full lips are slightly parted as she sleeps soundly. As I move beneath her, my rigid cock presses against her stomach, straining against my boxers.

"Dammit," I mutter.

I use my free hand to adjust myself, careful not to disturb her.

I'm not used to sharing a bed with someone. I never invite anyone back to my apartment. The women I've slept with know my terms—no strings attached, no misconceptions of a long-term commitment, and absolutely no cuddling.

Not only did I share a bed with Lila, but I broke my own rule. Although technically, she is on my side of the bed, which means I can't be held accountable for our snuggling.

I meant it when I told her that she's been on my mind since Andrew's engagement party. This woman has consumed my thoughts and has an uncanny ability to break through my defenses without even trying.

Lila's the last person I should be thinking about—not only is she my best friend's sister, but she's everything I'm not. She's an optimist who loves Christmas, believes in happily ever afters, and wants a life of adventure. I'm a skeptic who steers clear of commitment, avoids the holidays, and prefers the comfort of solitude.

Damn…way to get philosophical.

Everyone knew that my dad loved the holidays —and not just because our last name was Claus. He dressed up as Santa, decorated the Christmas tree with my grandma, and hosted a month-long Christmas movie marathon every December. Those were traditions I cherished, but after he passed, the magic was lost.

My body goes stiff when I feel the unmistakable warmth of breath against my cheek. Turning slowly, I come face to face with Winston, who's perched at the edge of the bed, eyeing me with a skeptical tilt of his head.

"Can I help you?" I whisper, my tone laced with sarcasm.

He blinks before repeatedly nudging my shoulder. I've never had a dog before, so I'm clueless as to what he wants. All I know is that if he keeps this up, he's going to disturb Lila, so it looks like we're stuck with each other for now.

I carefully maneuver out from under her, easing her arm from my hip so I can get up. I pause when she stirs, letting out a soft moan, but within seconds, her breathing evens out. She's spent every waking minute on Andrew's wedding and deserves the chance to sleep in when she can, especially since there's no telling how hectic the rest of the week will be.

Winston wags his tail as he darts to the ramp by the bed, and when he gets to the bottom, he sprints to the door. He starts whining, glancing back to see what's taking me so long.

"Calm down. I'm coming," I grumble.

For such a small dog, he's remarkably bossy.

I tiptoe across the room and ease the front door open, careful not to make too much noise. Without warning, Winston squeezes through the opening and barrels down the sidewalk and through the snow-covered yard.

He doesn't have a sweater on, and I'm not sure if he's allowed outside unsupervised. In my rush to follow him, I grab the first pair of slip-ons in sight—a pair of fuzzy pink slippers with bunny ears that look three sizes too small.

I hesitate, wondering if I should put my boots on instead, but Winston's barking makes the decision for me. I shove my feet into the slippers, the bunny ears bouncing with every step.

When I get outside, I hold my hand up to my face, squinting against the sunlight. When my eyes finally readjust, I see Winston running past the gate, heading toward the inn. *Dammit.*

I must have forgotten to close it last night. When he disappears from sight, I start sprinting, the icy air hitting my chest.

Fuck, it's cold.

In my hurry to chase Winston, I forgot to put on a shirt. Oh well, it's too late now.

As I get close to the inn, Winston's barking grows louder, and when he comes into view, I see that he's standing next to my grandma under a large tree where it looks like she's refilling one of her many bird feeders.

Naturally, of all days for her to be outside this early, it had to be today. I doubt her doctors would approve of her hauling a bag of birdseed around in the cold, but I know there's no chance of stopping her. I'm hoping once Jameson gets here, he'll have better luck convincing her to take it easy.

"What trouble are you up to so early, Winn?" Grandma crouches down and ruffles his fur affectionately.

She raises her head when I approach, a puzzled expression crossing her face. "Brooks? What in the world are you doing outside without a shirt?" She glances down at the bunny slippers. "I take it those don't belong to you." She straightens to her full height, arms folded, a playful smirk on her lips. "I noticed the storage room was empty this morning."

I narrow my eyes at her Cheshire grin. "Maybe if my cot hadn't busted last night, I'd have slept in there. It folded like a deck of cards. Any reason you had me use a faulty one?"

"Sounds like you had a rough night," she says sympathetically while dodging my question. "That doesn't explain why you're chasing Winston around wearing Lila's slippers. Don't think I didn't see you and her sneak off last night after dinner. Where did you go?" She taps her chin thoughtfully while studying me.

I shift uncomfortably, rubbing the back of my neck. Explaining to my grandma why I stayed at Lila's last night wasn't on the agenda for today.

"Her cottage. It's not a big deal," I mumble. "Nothing happened."

Grandma gives me a smug grin. "I never said it did. It's just interesting that you're up so early and without a shirt or shoes, no less. Are you planning on staying with her for the rest of your trip?"

It hadn't even occurred to me until now. After the cot disaster, just finding a place to sleep was my top priority. But now, the prospect of not staying with Lila for the remainder of my trip leaves a bitter taste in my mouth. Not that I'd tell Grandma that—hell, I don't even understand it myself.

"Has a room at the inn opened up?" I ask.

She shakes her head. "Nope. We're fully booked through the end of the year," she states without hesitation. The glint in her eye suggests she finds my predicament far too amusing for my liking.

"As much fun as it is standing out in the cold getting interrogated, I better get Winston back before Lila wakes up and worries when she realizes he's missing. The last thing I want is for her to think I've kidnapped her dog."

I scoop him into my arms and make my way back to the cottage. Winston gives me a disgruntled snort but eventually resigns himself to being stuck in air jail, resting his chin on my shoulder with a weary sigh.

"Tell Lila I say good morning," Grandma calls after me, her voice brimming with satisfaction.

I raise a hand in acknowledgment. My eyes are straight ahead, intent on getting back to the cottage as quickly as possible, not willing to chance Winston trying to make another break for it.

Now the question is, how am I going to explain this to Lila?

When Winston and I get inside, Lila is pacing the floor, her phone clutched in her hand.

She glances over, giving me a smile that doesn't reach her eyes. "I was wondering where you two wandered off to."

Winston trots up to her, whining softly as he rubs his head on her leg.

I shut the door behind me and stride over to her. "What's wrong?"

She sighs, running a hand across her face. "I just got off the phone with the owner of Bloom and Vine. They're pulling out of the wedding delivery on Christmas Day." She sinks onto the edge of the bed, her shoulders sagging. "I called to see if they had any white roses and hypericum berries—Hannah's favorites."

"And they didn't have any in stock?" I question.

My mind is already racing through my network, thinking of what connections I can leverage to get those flowers. Sure, I want Hannah and Andrew to have the flowers they want, but more than that, I want to make things easier for Lila. Whatever it takes, I'll do it.

"I wish that were the case." She drums her fingers against her thigh. "The florist was the one vendor the original bride had worked with directly. Her father already paid them in full and told them the wedding was canceled." She looks away, her gaze drifting to the window. "I explained the situation and offered to pay a rush fee for the new wedding flowers, but the owner said she was no longer interested in working on Christmas after being paid for the original order."

"Why don't you call another florist?"

She lets out a humorless laugh. "Bloom & Vine is the only one in the area. That's the trouble with being a wedding planner in a small town, there's no backup plan when a vendor decides to back out."

The stress rolls off her in waves, a palpable tension fills the room, and I have an urgency to fix this for her.

"We'll figure this out, alright?" I say, sitting down next to her.

She bites her lip, uncertainty flickering across her face. "We?"

"Yes." I nod. "We're in this together, aren't we? In case you forgot, you agreed to let me help with the wedding prep, so now you're stuck with me."

Acting on impulse, I pull her in for a hug with one arm wrapped around her shoulders, holding her tight as the other cradles the back of her head. She tenses at the unexpected gesture but relaxes into my embrace, circling her arms around my waist and resting her head against my chest. Having her this close seems inherently right, and while I'm supposed to be comforting her, it's hard to focus when all I can think about is how perfect she feels in my arms.

A fantasy plays in my mind of tugging her into my lap, her legs clinging to my waist with her hands tangled in my hair. I'd draw her closer, her soft lips brushing against mine. I swallow hard to suppress a groan. I clench my jaw, warding off the desire to grip the nape of her neck and bring her closer.

Lila looks like she's battling a similar storm of emotions, her lips slightly parted as if on the verge of surrendering to my touch.

God, this woman is messing with my head.

I clear my throat, withdrawing my hands from around her. "Call the florist back," I instruct.

A fleeting glimmer of disappointment flashes across her face before it vanishes.

"Why? What are you going to do?"

I lean in and tuck a stray piece of hair behind her and say, "Call them back, beautiful. Please let me help fix this."

After a short pause, she nods. "Okay."

With a resigned sigh, she grabs her phone from where she tossed it on the bed and dials the florist. I hold out my hand for the phone, and after hesitating briefly, she places it in my palm. I bring it to my ear, the tone ringing twice before someone picks up.

"Thanks for calling Bloom & Vine," a woman cheerfully answers. "This is Violet speaking. How may I help you?"

"Are you the owner, Violet?" I ask, cutting straight to the point.

She pauses a beat. "Yes, I am. What is this about?"

"My name is Brooks, Kay Claus's grandson. I believe she's a regular customer of yours. If I'm not mistaken, she orders weekly arrangements and uses Bloom & Vine for all events and weddings at the inn." I glance over at Lila, who's leaning closer and straining to hear both sides of the conversation.

"Absolutely. Whispering Pines Inn is one of our biggest clients. The team and I adore Kay."

"If that's the case, care to explain why you're refusing to make a delivery for a wedding taking place here on Christmas Day?"

"Mr. Claus," she says, her tone sharper now. "As I've already explained to Lila, we're no longer available to deliver on Christmas."

I pinch the bridge of my nose, irritated by her dismissive attitude. "If you agree to do the flowers for the Christmas wedding, I'll throw in ten grand for your trouble. Is that enough to change your mind?" I look over to see Lila waving her arms wildly, an alarmed expression on her face.

"Are you messing with me?" Violet sputters.

"No, I don't have time for games," I state.

"Okay, you've got a deal. I must admit, you drive a hard bargain," she says. "My employees and I will appreciate the bonus."

"You're not going to keep it all for yourself?" I ask, a little surprised.

"My team is like family, Mr. Claus. I make sure they're well taken care of, especially when they're away from their loved ones on Christmas morning."

"Have the flowers here by 10:00 a.m. on Christmas morning, and I'll have the bonus waiting," I say, my chest tightening. I rub my palm against it. Must be indigestion.

"Yes, of course. It was nice doing business with you, Mr. Claus."

"Goodbye, Violet." I hang up without waiting for a response. There's nothing more to discuss since she's agreed, and there's no chance she'll bail with ten thousand dollars on the line. Scratch that, I'll make it twenty thousand...considering she's splitting it with her staff.

"Bloom & Vine will do the flowers," I inform Lila, handing back her phone.

She pushes her hair over her shoulder with a frustrated sigh. "Why would you do that?" she exclaims.

"I think what you meant to say is 'thank you,'" I reply with a smirk.

"For what? Bribing the local florist. Thank you, Brooks, for setting an unrealistic precedent that whenever I need flowers at an inconvenient time, they'll expect an extra ten grand," she replies dryly.

I narrow my eyes. "I did what was necessary to guarantee

Hannah and Andrew have the flowers they want at their wedding. Trust me, the money isn't a concern."

"Not all of us can afford to throw cash around like it's confetti." She shakes her head, exasperated.

I frown. "Why are you upset? We had a problem, and I took care of it. Isn't that what you wanted? For me to help you fix any issues that come up?"

She gathers her hair and sweeps it over one shoulder, giving me a measured look. "Brooks, I appreciate what you were trying to do, but I've worked hard to build relationships with local vendors, and throwing money around complicates things for me in the long run. Particularly since Violet loves to gossip, and she'll tell every other vendor in town to expect sky-high premiums for holiday and rush orders moving forward."

"I won't let that happen."

"What are you going to do? Throw more money at the problem?"

"You say that like it's a bad thing."

Lila eyes me suspiciously as I cross the room and grab my phone from the kitchenette counter before coming back to stand next to her. With a few swift taps, I send a text to my assistant, directing him to call Violet at Bloom & Vine back and explain that we'll double the bonus to deliver the flowers on Christmas if she promises to keep that detail to herself. I already decided to give her team twenty grand, but it doesn't hurt to make sure Lila benefits from it too.

Owning a studio has its advantages, like knowing how to leverage negotiation tactics when the situation calls for it, and this is one of those times where discretion is key. The last thing I want to do is complicate Lila's relationships with local vendors, and this is the best way to ensure Violet keeps the details of our transaction to herself.

"Done," I announce triumphantly. "My assistant will reach

out to Violet within ten minutes and remind her that we want to make sure her team is fairly compensated working on Christmas, but that discretion is non-negotiable in return."

I skip the details about the double bonus. There's no reason for adding fuel to the fire. The flowers will be here on time, and that's what matters most.

"How about when the next problem comes up, we discuss it before you go full-on CEO mode?" Lila says, crossing her arms.

"You think we'll have more fires to put out before the big day?"

She nods, her lips curling into a wry smile. "I'm counting on it. For every crisis averted, there's three more lying in wait. The job of a wedding planner isn't finished until a couple is hitched and off on their honeymoon."

"Well, I guess I better keep my credit card close," I joke.

I'm stunned when she leans over to kiss me on the cheek.

"What was that for?"

"For saving the day and for making sure Hannah has the flowers she wants on her wedding day. Your tactics may be questionable, but I appreciate it all the same." She casts me an amused glance when I fold my arms across my chest. "Hold on. Did you go outside without a shirt?" She bursts out laughing as she scans me from head to toe. "And are those my bunny slippers?" She points to the offending footwear still on my feet.

"Winston had to go out, and I didn't want to wake you," I explain, dodging her question. "When I opened the door, he bolted, and I had to chase him."

Lila tilts her head, studying me. "By chance did you leave the gate open last night?"

"Maybe, but in my defense, I had a suitcase. Rest assured, I'll be more careful next time. There's no way I'm risking my grandma seeing me like that again—she was far too entertained."

Lila holds out her hand, eyes wide with shock. "Wait. Kay

saw you like this…" She motions at me. "While you were chasing *my* dog?"

I nod. "She was out refilling her bird feeders, and Winston ran to her before I could catch him. Safe to say, she found my predicament rather amusing."

"Oh my god." Lila covers her face with her hands. "You realize she'll never let us live this down, right? I can only imagine what she thinks happened last night, seeing you half-dressed after leaving my cottage."

I take a step closer, my voice low. "Tell me, Goldie, what would she assume we did last night?"

Lila hesitates, her throat bobbing. "You know exactly what I mean."

I shrug. "Why don't you spell it out for me anyway."

"Your grandma probably thinks we slept together," she blurts out.

"We did."

She lets out an exasperated sigh, narrowing her eyes. "No, I mean she probably thinks we…you know, had sex." Her voice drops.

There's something irresistibly charming about seeing her get flustered. Her cheeks turn a soft pink as she nibbles on her lower lip.

I meet her gaze with a smirk. "And would that be so bad? You're the one who admitted to having a crush on me, remember."

"*Had* being the operative word. If we ever did sleep together—which we're not—it isn't something I'd go around telling Kay. She's your grandma, for heaven's sake."

I let the silence stretch on.

Like sunlight breaking through a gray sky, she draws me toward her warmth, impossible to ignore. The space between us feels like a chasm I'm desperate to close, even though I have every reason to hold back. Lila is a burst of sunshine with an endless supply of holiday cheer, while I'm the skeptical grinch, masking my vulnerability with calculated indifference.

Yet that doesn't stop me from accepting her challenge by cupping her chin with my hand and tilting her face to meet my gaze. Her breath hitches when I bring my mouth close to hers, leaving barely an inch of space between us. I can feel her hot breath against my lips like a whisper. She grabs hold of the waistband of my sweatpants like her body craves for me to come closer, yet her mind screams to push me away. Her nails lightly brush my hip, lingering there as her chest rises sharply, her breathing unsteady, betraying her internal conflict.

She tilts her head back slightly, her pulse visible in the delicate curve of her throat.

"You're right," I whisper, breathing in her ear. "You're completely unaffected by me. What a shame." A whimper escapes her as I step back, and I can't help but suppress a smirk.

Looks like she's not as indifferent as she'd like me to believe.

"For someone who says we should keep our distance, you can't seem to keep your hands off of me. It's ironic, don't you think," she retorts.

She makes a fair point. Whether or not I'm ready to admit it, Lila Monroe has the power to turn my entire world upside down if I let her.

"You're not exactly making it easy to give you space. Why is that?" I ask.

She shrugs, but the way her fingers twitch betrays her calm exterior. "When I figure that out, I'll let you know."

Her response hints that I'm not the only one grappling with what's happening between us.

"What's on the agenda today, Goldie?" I ask, wanting to change the subject. "I'm all yours, so put me to work."

CHAPTER 7

AFTER MY UNEXPECTEDLY EVENTFUL MORNING, I TOOK a quick shower and rushed to the inn. It's past noon and I'm in the events room starting to set up decorations for the wedding. We don't have any other events until then, so it gives me plenty of time to make sure every detail is in order.

My phone buzzes, the sound echoing throughout the mostly empty room.

Fallon: Girl! I just looked up Brooks Claus. He's hot AF!

Fallon: Is he as good of a kisser as you remember? He definitely looks like it.

Lila: OMG! I told you nothing happened. He's only staying with me because the inn is fully booked.

She called an hour ago to check in, and I looped her in on the Brooks' situation.

Fallon: You've had a crush on this man since you were a teenager. This is your chance to act on it.

Lila: Oh sure, because going after my brother's best friend sounds like a great plan.

Fallon: Life is short. What's worse, risking it or regretting you never took the chance later?

Lila: Don't you have a hockey stick to bedazzle?

Fallon: I couldn't decide between red rhinestones or silver glitter.

Fallon: I think I'll use both.

Lila: Am I going to have to fly out there and intervene when Harrison gets back?

Fallon: I can handle him on my own, thank you very much.

Lila: You're not the one I'm worried about.

Fallon: Ha. Ha. Very funny.

Lila: I'm going to finish decorating, but we'll chat later, okay?

Fallon: You can count on it.

I put my phone on a nearby chair and grab a strand of garland and the mistletoe I want to hang above the archway.

Before I can get back to work, Brooks strides into the event hall like he owns the place, dressed in dark wash jeans and a white button-down shirt. He's the epitome of sex appeal, and I swear he somehow gets more attractive every time I see him, although I'd be lying if I said I wasn't a little disappointed that he's fully dressed.

Curiosity gets the better of me when he crouches down beside Winston, who's sulking near the doorway. Kay had to run some errands, and my parents stopped by Dad's office, so Winston has been stuck with me while I worked. Given his theatrical response, you'd think he was being punished.

Brooks extends his hand toward Winston, holding a slice of ham in his palm. "I got you a treat from the kitchen, buddy. After your jailbreak this morning, I figured a truce might be in order."

Winston barely sniffs the ham before nudging the offending meat away with his nose. I should tell Brooks that chicken, peanut butter biscuits, or whipped cream are the only ways to win Winston over, but I keep quiet, thoroughly enjoying the sight of my finicky dog giving him a run for his money.

"Seriously?" Brooks groans. "It's freshly sliced ham. What's the problem?" He gives it another shot, but Winston rests his paw on Brooks' hand and pushes him away before sitting back on his haunches, giving Brooks the side eye.

With a defeated sigh, Brooks tosses the ham into the trash can. "Alright, I get it; you're a food connoisseur. There's no need to be such a snob about it," he grumbles.

Winston glances over at me with a look that says, *"How much longer do I have to put up with this guy?"*

Something tells me he wouldn't be happy if he knew I've been hoping Brooks might stick around longer.

I put my hand on my hip in mock irritation, shooting Brooks a playful glare. "Did you just call my dog a snob?"

Brooks points to Winston. "He started it," he argues. "I suggested a truce, but he wasn't having it."

I raise a brow. "He's a dog."

"Oh, come on. He knows exactly what he's doing," Brooks

adds. He narrows his eyes at Winston, who tilts his head toward me, wagging his tail, feigning ignorance.

"I'm going to let the two of you sort this out," I say with a chuckle.

I go back to winding garland across one side of the archway I'm decorating, making sure each loop falls evenly, creating a cascading effect that will frame the space perfectly. I've learned from years of experience that perfection is in the details, and I'll never settle for less.

Maybe that's why I'm still single. My standards for a partner are high, and I'm in the habit of ending things after a few dates when there's no spark, no matter how much I wish there was.

Having worked with countless couples, I've developed an instinct for predicting who will last and who won't. For every couple who navigates life together, there's another who's barely hanging on, caught in a cycle of misunderstandings and disappointments.

I'm waiting for someone who wants to create a life together, strive toward our shared dreams, and looks at me like I'm his entire universe.

Don't get me wrong—I'm a firm believer in happily ever after. Not in the way most people think of them, complete with glass slippers and fairy godmothers, but in the idea that love can be transformative. I've witnessed firsthand that once people find their other half, their entire world shifts. It's why I fell in love with wedding planning. Sure, I enjoy organizing all types of events, but there's something special about being part of a couple's big day.

My favorite moment of any wedding is when the groom catches his first glimpse of the bride walking down the aisle. In that instant, everything around him disappears, and all that matters is the woman he'll vow to love and cherish forever.

Weddings are all about the little details, I remind myself while staring up at the archway. I realize even with a step stool, I can't quite reach the center to secure the mistletoe. Undeterred, I stretch up on my tiptoes, teetering on the stool as my fingers barely skim the edge of the archway.

"Dammit, Lila. What the hell are you doing?" Brooks exclaims with alarm. "You're going to get hurt."

He steps toward me despite me waving him off. "I'm fine. I do this all the time," I say

To be fair, I usually have a ladder when I'm decorating the event hall, but the crew from Snowy Mountain Stables borrowed it last month and haven't returned it. So I'm left improvising with a rickety step stool I found in the maintenance closet, which wouldn't be an issue if I were taller.

With determination, I sweep my hair away from my face, set on doing this on my own. "Come on, just a little higher," I mutter as I lean forward. "Almost there," I breathe as I close the final distance. Once I've secured the mistletoe, I smile in triumph, but it's short-lived when the stool shifts beneath me, and my stomach drops as I fight to regain my balance to no avail. A gasp escapes my lips, and I close my eyes, bracing myself for the inevitable fall.

Instead of hitting the ground, I'm scooped into strong arms and pulled into a solid chest. "I've got you," Brooks says, his voice calm and steady.

My hands cling to his shoulders as he exhales slowly. He strides to the closet chair, taking a seat with me still in his lap. He briefly closes his eyes, his chest rising and falling against mine, and I'm hyper-aware of the warmth radiating from him and the way my body seems to fit perfectly against his.

"Thank you for saving me," I say softly.

"You need to be more careful," he snaps.

"Someone's back to being grumpy," I sass back.

"You call it grumpy; I call it concern," he grumbles, letting out a deep breath. "I don't want to see you get hurt," he says as he brushes back a piece of my hair and tucks it behind my ear.

My heart is racing for an entirely different reason now. My

mind is reeling from the fact that Brooks Claus has me in his arms, and I admit I don't want him to let me go.

"The mistletoe looks good, doesn't it?" My voice comes out breathy and uneven.

"Yes, it looks nice. But let's not make a habit of you falling for decorations, okay?" His eyes search mine, his grip on my waist firm as if he's afraid to let me go. "You're far more important than some mistletoe." My pulse quickens when he flashes me a crooked smile.

He keeps this carefree version of himself under lock and key, and it's impossible to ignore how much it means that he's showing it to me.

I can't control my fleeting thoughts of what it might be like to kiss him under the mistletoe. Visions of him gazing at me with those chocolate brown eyes as he traces my jawline torment me, wishing it were real.

"Lila, can you remind me what time the sleigh ride—"

I whip my head around to see Kay standing in the doorway, a broad smile lighting up her face. "Am I interrupting?"

Oh my gosh.

I scramble out of Brooks' lap, smoothing my shirt in a futile attempt to hide that I'm flustered. It feels like we're middle schoolers getting caught alone with our crush for the first time. Based on Kay's gaze lingering on us, she's not the least bit bothered by the fact that she just caught me sitting in her grandson's lap.

Brooks clears his throat as he stands up. "Grandma, what are you doing here?"

She raises a brow, hands on her hips. "Last I checked, this is my inn. Did I miss the memo where I need your permission to walk around freely?" she asks, her tone teasing.

He shakes his head. "No, of course not. You just said you'd be gone for a few hours."

"I finished early and thought I'd see if Lila needed some help, but it looks like you have it covered," she smirks. "Sorry to interrupt. I'll be at the front desk if you need me." She heads down the hall without a second glance, Winston trailing after her.

Brooks walks over to the pile of garland waiting to be strung and picks up a handful.

"What are you doing?"

"There's no way I'm letting you hang anything else and risk falling again. Now, are you going to direct me or risk me doing it wrong?" he dares, grabbing the step stool and carrying it underneath the wooden beam on the far side of the room.

For the next few hours, it's just me and Brooks surrounded by the lights and garland as we decorate. We talk and laugh, the conversation flowing naturally. There's something so easy about being with him, and having him here feels like home in a way I can't explain.

The sun is low in the sky as our group gathers outside, bundled in our warmest coats and scarves. The air is filled with laughter as everyone chats amongst themselves. I have my binder open to the guest list, making sure everyone who signed up for the sleigh ride is here. Since Andrew and Hannah's wedding party is small, I was able to extend an invitation to the guests who wanted to participate.

The Snowy Mountain Stables are a short walk from the inn, making it an ideal activity for any time of year. Although for me, nothing compares to the magic of a sleigh ride over Mistletoe Ridge in the winter.

I'm halfway through reviewing the list when movement at the front entrance of the inn catches my attention.

I glance up just in time to watch Brooks step outside.

After we finished decorating the events room, he went back

to my cottage to get ready while I finished prep for the activity tonight.

He must have taken a shower because he's clean-shaven, and his hair neatly styled aside from a strand falling loose near his temple. He's wearing a gray wool coat layered over a cable-knit sweater, dark jeans, and boots. He exudes an air of confidence that captivates everyone around him, including a group of women waiting for the sleigh ride, who are transfixed by him as if he's the ultimate catch.

A knot of jealousy tightens in my stomach when one of them waves at Brooks, flashing him a smile when he looks in her direction. He walks past them, unaffected by their stares, his focus already shifted elsewhere.

Sharing a bed for one night doesn't make him mine, so why does the mere idea of him being with someone else make my blood run hot? His lack of interest in her advances is the one bright spot, making me think there's a chance for more between us.

The clip-clop of hooves echoing in the distance breaks through my thoughts, and seconds later, several horse-drawn sleighs come around the corner. Each sleigh is painted black, decorated with garland and a red bow, and features three wide benches lined with plush seats and plaid blankets to keep everyone warm.

Hannah claps her hands together as they pull up to the inn. "Oh, Lila, you've truly outdone yourself," she exclaims. "This is amazing."

"Yeah, sis, this is incredible." Andrew wraps an arm around me in a side hug. "Thanks for doing this."

"It's my pleasure."

I mean it. This is why I love being a wedding planner—creating unforgettable moments for my clients. This time, it's extra special being able to do something for the people I love. In years past, Andrew and Hannah scheduled a sleigh ride when they were town, so I wanted to make sure this was part of their wedding experience.

Michael, the driver of the first sleigh, gives me a wave. "We're ready when you are, Lila."

I wave back with a smile. "Perfect, thanks." I turn around to face the group. "Alright, time to climb aboard, everybody," I say, gesturing toward the sleighs. "There are enough blankets for everyone, and when you get back, there will be refreshments waiting for you in the lobby. Have fun."

As my dad, Aunt Tilly, and Uncle Ted file into the closest sleigh, my mom stops next to me and places a hand on my arm. "Are you coming, Lila?"

"If there's enough room. I just want to make sure everyone else has a seat first."

She gives me a pat on the cheek. "Alright. You work so hard, and I want to make sure you enjoy yourself too."

I give her a reassuring smile. "I will, don't worry."

She nods, satisfied with my answer, and climbs in next to my dad. That's when I notice Andrew and Hannah have already settled in the sleigh ahead of the one my parents are in.

"Andrew, wait," I shout to get his attention.

He spins around in his seat. "What is it?"

"I arranged for you and Hannah to have your own private ride. It's right over there." I gesture to a two-seater sleigh that's just pulling up behind the others.

He flashes me a grin as the one he's in starts gliding forward. "Looks like we're along for the ride in this one. I'm sure there's another couple who would love a romantic experience. See you when we get back." After a quick wave, he faces forward, wrapping his arm around Hannah as she rests her head on his shoulder.

As I look around, I realize everyone else has already boarded.

"Well shoot," I mutter as I close my planner.

"What's the matter?" Brooks' low voice catches me off guard as he pushes off the wall where he'd been leaning.

"You're still here? I figured you'd already gotten on with everyone else. Let me guess, sleigh rides aren't your thing?" I taunt him.

He gives an amused chuckle. "Actually, I wanted to make sure I stuck around in case you needed help with anything."

"Oh."

He stayed behind for me?

It's the last thing I expected, but I have to admit, it's unexpectedly sweet of him.

"What are you two still standing around for?" Kay interjects, stepping outside with Winston on her heels.

"I was making sure no one got left behind," I answer lamely.

"You did your job perfectly." She waves around to the empty parking lot. "It looks like there's one sleigh left, so you and Brooks should get a move on." She comes over, takes the binder from me, and tucks it under her arm.

I furrow my brow. "Aren't you coming?"

She shakes her head. "Winston and I are going to get him a treat from the kitchen, and we'll be here waiting with hot chocolate and a fresh batch of gingerbread cookies when you get back." She lifts him up in her other arm. "Oh, and Brooks, glad to see you didn't try to brave the snow again in Lila's slippers. They might be cute, but they aren't ideal for the outdoors," she teases as she heads back inside. "Have fun, kids," she adds over her shoulder before the door shuts behind her.

"Think she'll ever let you forget about wearing my bunny slippers?" I ask Brooks with a grin.

"Not a chance," he mutters with a rueful smile. "She's right though. We better get a move on."

He doesn't wait for a response, ushering me toward the waiting sleigh, where the driver is settled in his seat. "Jump in," the driver urges before putting on a pair of headphones and staring straight ahead.

Brooks steps closer, extending his hand toward me. When I take it, an electric charge buzzes between us, and everything else fades away. As he helps me into the carriage, his thumb grazes my knuckles, sending a thrill down my spine, and my pulse races out of control.

His touch lingers even after I'm seated, his smoldering gaze holding me captive. It's as if time stands still, and we're the only two people in the universe sharing a connection deeper than words.

"Are you coming?" I whisper, afraid to break the spell hanging between us like a thread.

"There's nowhere else I'd rather be." He gives my hand a gentle squeeze before climbing in beside me.

Maybe this connection between us isn't just in my head after all.

As the sleigh moves forward, I can feel it in my bones—the next hour could either become one of the highlights of my life or a crushing letdown that I may never recover from.

CHAPTER 8

WE RIDE IN SILENCE AS WE GO PAST A TRAIL DOTTED with fir trees and bare birches dusted with a layer of snow, their branches bending toward each other to create a canopy that glitters in the fading light. The crisp air carries the scent of pine and cedar, and the only sound is the steady clop of hooves and the occasional jingling of bells tied to the horses' harnesses.

When my family visited Starlight Pines in the winter, we'd go sledding, have epic snowball fights, and I'd hang with Andrew at his house. Surprisingly enough, we never took a sleigh ride, so I'm taking in the scenery around me for the first time.

Lila sits beside me with the blanket on her lap, her gaze lingering on the snowy canopy, a serene smile on her face.

I'm entranced by her presence, from her infectious smile to the way she chews on her lip when she's nervous, and I'm struck by how easily she quiets the storm inside me. And her love for the holidays has me seeing this time of year in a whole new light, making it impossible not to get swept up in her excitement.

Admittedly, some of my thoughts are far from innocent. It's been hours, but I can't shake the memory of us in the events room.

Her body pressed tightly to mine as I held her close, the sweet scent of peppermint swirling around us, and the unmistakable hunger in her eyes as they lingered on my mouth.

When I glance over again, I notice she's shivering, and her teeth are chattering.

Without thinking, I scoot closer and drape an arm around her, pulling her into my embrace. Even through all the layers, I can feel her warmth, and I will myself to banish the inappropriate thoughts.

"What are you doing?" Lila asks, wide-eyed.

"Can't have you turning into an icicle on my watch now, can I?" I say, tucking the blanket tighter around her legs.

She tilts her head, the corner of her mouth twitching like she's fighting a smirk. "I rather like chivalrous Brooks."

"It's called self-preservation. If you catch hypothermia, I'm the one who has to explain to Andrew why his sister got sick on my watch."

"And here I thought you were just being sweet," she quips.

I hold her extra close as I recall the way everything seemed to slow down as she lost her balance and fell off the stool earlier today—it was only a few feet off the ground, but she could have been seriously injured if I hadn't been there to catch her.

The idea of her getting hurt sends a sharp pain through my chest, sparking an overwhelming need to draw her into my arms and reassure myself she's safe.

Despite my best efforts to keep my walls up, she is dismantling them brick by brick, and the more I try to convince myself she's off-limits and push her from my mind, the stronger my desire for her becomes.

Which leaves me confused.

I've built a successful empire by devoting my life to my business and shutting my emotions out. If I don't allow myself to feel,

I don't have to face the complications they bring. Yet none of that holds true with Lila.

Begging the question, would my priorities shift if I had something—or *someone*—that I cared about to come home to at night? *Someone like her.*

"Is something wrong?" Lila rests her hand on my cheek, her face shadowed with worry.

I nod. "I'm fine."

"Good." She smiles. "I was beginning to think you regret being stuck in a sleigh with me."

She's wrong.

Her presence is magnetic, and I'm drawn to her like a moth to a flame.

I shake my head. "Never." I lift her other hand from under the blanket and bring them both to my mouth to warm them, the tips of her fingers ice cold against my lips. "You've somehow made the holiday season bearable again, believe it or not," I say, voicing my earlier thoughts.

"What do you mean?" Sadness clouds her expression, a reflection of her empathy that makes me want to confide in her.

"Christmas was my dad's favorite holiday, which is why we always celebrated in Starlight Pines. He said our apartment in New York was too cold and impersonal, and this was the only place that captured the spirit of the season, and he wanted my brothers and me to experience that too." I pause, my eyes drifting to the snow-covered trees. "He was the glue that kept our family together, and after he died, the thought of celebrating the holidays without him felt like a betrayal, let alone coming back to the place that reminded me of his absence."

"I'm so sorry, Brooks," Lila says with a downcast gaze. "I can't imagine how hard it is to be here, especially during the holidays."

I lower our hands into my lap. "It wasn't fair of me to stay away, especially when my grandma was left to grieve alone while my brothers and I avoided coming back. She deserves better."

"Kay hasn't been alone." Lila's words ease the guilt pressing against my chest. "She gave me my dream job despite my lack of experience, trusting I would grow into the role. Learning from her has been a privilege, and I cherish every opportunity to return her kindness."

"I meant it when I said my grandma is lucky to have you." I swallow the lump in my throat.

She's not the only one.

Lila shifts in her seat. "Brooks," she whispers.

"Yeah?"

"I might only be your friend's annoying little sister, but I'm here if you ever want to talk. You never have to be alone if you don't want to be."

And just like that, she's managed to dismantle the notion of keeping her at arm's length. She doesn't owe me anything, and yet, she's offered me compassion and patience—things I'm not sure I deserve.

"Bullshit," I state in a hushed tone. "You're so much more than Andrew's sister. You're thoughtful and funny and an incredible event planner. This wedding wouldn't have been possible without you. You've become my grandmother's favorite person—aside from Winston, of course. Not to mention, you're beautiful inside and out, and I admire how much you care about those around you."

Lila laughs, shaking her head. "Is that a line from one of your movies?"

"Nope, it's the truth."

She pauses, opening her mouth to add something, but stops herself.

When we turn off onto a dirt road, she points to a sign that says *Welcome to Mistletoe Ridge.*

"We're here," she exclaims.

I arch a brow, scanning our surroundings. "Where exactly is *here,* and why is it called Mistletoe Ridge?"

"You'll see," she says with a twinkle in her eye.

I don't notice anything out of the ordinary until she edges closer, nudging me lightly. "Look up." Her breath grazes the side of my neck as she speaks.

When I do what she asks, my mouth falls open when I spot the hundreds of clusters of mistletoe suspended from the branches of the surrounding oak and pine trees. The white berries are a sharp contrast to the green leaves, and it's hard to believe they're real.

How did I not know this place existed before today? I've been to Starlight Pines dozens of times, but I guess as a kid, visiting a landmark that I'd assume is considered romantic was the last thing on my mind. And once I got old enough to date, I can only imagine this would have been the last spot my dad and grandma would have wanted to put on my radar.

"The view is absolutely incredible, isn't it?" Lila asks, her gaze drifting upward.

"You're right," I reply, never looking away from her. "It's unlike anything I've ever seen. I'd go as far as to say it's the most stunning thing I've ever laid eyes on."

"Don't tell me you're going soft over a little mistletoe…" She laughs, but the sound fades when she notices my focus is entirely on her, the view being the furthest thing from my mind.

Our faces are mere inches apart, my pulse speeds up as I absentmindedly trace my finger along her jawline, silently counting the freckles scattered across her cheeks. Lila trembles under my touch but doesn't pull away.

There's a smudge of lip gloss on the side of her mouth, and I gently wipe it off with the pad of my thumb. Her breath hitches in response, her plump lips practically begging to be kissed.

"Do you have a thing for my mouth or something?" she teases softly.

"I have a thing for *you*," I confess in a whisper.

She tilts her head back, eyes wide. "Please don't say that if you don't mean it."

"You should know by now that I don't say things I don't mean, Goldie."

Right now, everything that should hold me back from wanting her fades into the background.

My mind is consumed with the need to close the distance between us. We're under a forest full of mistletoe, like the fates are conspiring to make me forget why I've been holding back.

It's only one kiss; what's the worst that could happen?

That thought may come back to haunt me later, but right now, I couldn't care less.

For once, I abandon the thought entirely, leaning in to press a chaste kiss to her collarbone. She melts into my touch as I trail kisses up her neck, along her jaw, and when I finally skim my lips over hers, sending a heat spreading through me like wildfire, I can't get enough.

Lila nips my bottom lip, delving her tongue inside my mouth. *She tastes like mint and sunshine.*

I never expected kissing her would be like this—electric, urgent, and leaving me craving more.

"God, you're so beautiful," I murmur.

"And you're halfway charming without that perpetual frown on your face," she teases, her fingers trailing along the outline of my mouth.

I capture her hand, pressing a kiss to her palm. "Careful, Goldie, or you might make me believe you actually enjoy my—"

Before I can finish, the sound of distant laughter and muffled conversation drifts toward us, shattering the stillness like a dropped glass. Lila's cheeks flush a deeper shade, and as she retreats to her side of the sleigh, her hand brushes my thigh. I inhale deeply, reining in the desire to keep her close, and lean my head back, wondering how I became so enthralled with this woman.

"We must be near the lake," she says, craning her neck for a better view. "All the sleighs stop so the guests can take in the view."

And just like that, the absence of her body against mine leaves a void colder than the wind nipping at my face.

We're the last to get back to the inn.

Lila immediately shifts back into hostess mode when she spots the guests milling around the lobby and helps my grandma pass out cups of hot chocolate and shortbread.

I'm struck by how effortlessly she can switch gears from sharing a private moment together in a sleigh to slipping into the role of hostess like it's second nature. It's not just her efficiency but also the way she manages to make everyone feel welcome, and seems to brighten the room with her presence.

Returning to Starlight Pines has turned out to be nothing like I expected it would. I've avoided coming back because it reminded me of what I lost, and I wanted to avoid celebrating the holidays at all costs. But now, I'm starting to think this town might hold more for me than the ghosts of the past and could be the start of a new beginning.

What should have been a quick visit to check on my grandma has evolved into finding a reason to stay past Christmas so I can spend more time with Lila. The endless pile of paperwork and scripts waiting on my desk in California no longer seem as pressing as they used to be.

What terrifies me the most is how I'm consumed by an insatiable longing to kiss her again.

Whether I'm ready to admit it or not, she has the power to change everything, and I can't help but wonder—what would happen if I let her not only into my life but also my heart?

I shake my head in an attempt to banish the silly notion, but it refuses to leave.

Andrew joins me by the fireplace with a mug of hot chocolate in hand, and a frown etched across his face.

"Careful, Andrew, or that scowl will be stuck like that for your wedding photos," I mutter.

He crosses his free arm across his chest, his pointed stare locked in on me. "Care to tell me why you're looking at my sister like she's the only person in the room? Or better yet, why you're staying in her cottage? You didn't mention it when we talked earlier."

My ears burn, but I keep my expression neutral. I take a long sip of my drink, buying myself time to think.

He's right. I've purposely avoided the subject. What was I supposed to tell him? That Lila has dominated my thoughts for the past four months, and now that she's slipped past my defenses, it's as if a dam has broken, and there's no stopping the tide from rushing in.

"Well?" Andrew drums his fingers against his leg, waiting for my reply.

"All the rooms were booked, so I was sleeping in the storage room, but my cot broke last night."

He snorts. "And my sister's cottage was the *only* place you could stay? That's convenient."

"Need I remind you that you're the one who volunteered me to help her with the wedding?"

"Last time I checked, staying at Lila's place wasn't part of being my best man," he retorts.

Technically, we shared a bed, and even though nothing happened, it seems like something I should keep to myself. The last thing I want is to give Andrew more reason to be suspicious of my intentions.

Which begs the question: *What are my intentions when it comes to Lila?*

There was always the option of sleeping on the floor in my grandma's room or crashing on one of the couches in the lobby. Granted, neither option would have been particularly comfortable, and the latter could have caused guests to report me to the front desk for loitering.

The truth is, I couldn't resist Lila's invitation to stay with her when the opportunity presented itself. Not taking the chance would have haunted me, just like I regret walking away from her at the engagement party, and I wasn't about to make the same mistake twice.

Andrew's eyes narrow as he leans against the mantle. "Is there something going on between you and my sister?"

"Nothing happened last night," I answer, deflecting the question.

I avoid telling him about the kiss Lila and I shared at Mistletoe Ridge earlier—another detail I doubt he'd take kindly to hearing. He's my best friend, and I'm afraid of how this will affect our relationship. He's privy to every detail of my past and has been my wingman since we were teenagers, well aware of my lack of commitment to the women I've hooked up with. Lila is one of the most important people in his life, and I worry he'll assume I'm taking advantage of her because of our forced proximity.

"I'm not sure that..."

I trail off when Hannah approaches. "Andrew, there you are," she says with a smile. "Your mom was hoping to introduce us to a friend of hers who recently moved to town."

I let out a breath of relief, grateful for the interruption. That's the problem with having a best friend since childhood. He knows all your secrets.

Yes, I want Lila, but risking my friendship with Andrew and Hannah for something I'm still trying to figure out seems reckless. And the last thing I want is to cast a shadow over their big day. But even now, I can't shake the pull I have toward Lila, and I can only hope that Andrew doesn't see what I'm trying so hard to hide—that every time I look at his sister, it feels like the ground shifts beneath me.

I'm diving headfirst into uncharted territory, and every minute spent with Lila makes it harder to hold back. Our kiss under the mistletoe is now etched in my memory, and I'm not sure I'll

be able to stop myself from falling for her. *I'm halfway there already.*

CHAPTER 9

Lila

When I wake up the next morning, Brooks has already left for the gym, and the sun is filtering through the curtains. He didn't get back to the cottage until after I was already in bed, leaving me anxious that we haven't had the chance to talk about what happened last night.

Tomorrow is Christmas, and while my mind should be on the final touches so the wedding goes off without a hitch, my thoughts are on Brooks.

I bury my face into my pillow, replaying our magical kiss beneath a canopy of mistletoe, something that'll forever be etched into my memory. I swear I can still feel the whisper of his breath lingering against my skin, his hands cradling my face, and the quiet intensity in his eyes as if to say he'd been waiting for that moment as much as I had.

Never in my wildest dreams did I think Brooks Claus would look at me that way, especially after years of believing my crush on him would always be hopelessly one-sided.

In the past few days, I've glimpsed a side of him hidden from most. Behind his gruff exterior, he's surprisingly attentive, considerate, and, dare I say, even sweet. Like when he adjusted the blanket during the sleigh ride to make sure I stayed warm.

My mind is a jumbled mess, so I text the one person who I can count on to say what I need to hear—or at least distract me enough to clear my head.

Lila: I might have done something I shouldn't have done last night.

Fallon: Did you finally have sex with Brooks?

Lila: What? No.

Lila: He kissed me during a sleigh ride to Mistletoe Ridge.

Fallon: OMG. I knew it!

Fallon: How was it?

Lila: Magical.

Fallon: Girl, I'm totally catering your wedding.

Lila: Will you stop? Just because we kissed doesn't mean it'll lead to anything else.

Fallon: Oh, please. He's totally smitten with you.

Lila: And you know this how?

Fallon: I have a sixth sense for these things.

Lila: We live on opposite sides of the country. It would never work.

I set my phone on the nightstand and lie back in bed.

Maybe Fallon is onto something with the whole new adventure concept, though it seems easier said than done. She's definitely braver than me—when she decided she wanted a change, she spontaneously packed up her life in London and moved to the U.S. I don't think I could make that kind of leap, especially not across the ocean.

Like me, my parents tend to stick close to home. Growing up, our vacations were mainly in Vermont, with the occasional visit to New Hampshire to see relatives and a class trip I took to New York City for graduation. It's a cruel twist of fate that Brooks lives on the other side of the country. Why couldn't he be in New England or even New York? Either would be far more reasonable than California.

I assumed that the temporary nature of his stay would serve as a reminder to temper my attraction, but it only makes it burn brighter.

Wanting to take the edge off, I slip out of bed and tiptoe to the bathroom. Winston is still asleep in his dog bed, so I leave the door slightly ajar in case he wakes up before I'm done.

After I open the glass door to the shower and turn it on, I strip out of my pajamas and step under the stream of hot water. I'm thrumming with need as I step under the spray, wound up like a spring and unable to wait any longer for my next release. I nibble on my lower lip, my gaze shifting to the door. The last thing I should be worried about is getting off, but this could be my only chance of being alone today.

One little orgasm can't hurt, right?

With my mind made up, I take the shower head from its holder, setting the spray to a pulsing stream. Every breath is heavy with restless energy as I prop my right leg to rest on the tiled ledge of the shower and position the shower head between my legs. I close my eyes as the rapid pulses hit my core, and the spray echoes off the walls. A fantasy takes shape as the pressure builds.

Brooks and I are back in the sleigh. He kisses me with urgency like he's been craving this for days. His focus is on my mouth, but I'm keenly aware of his hand sliding under the blanket. I gasp when he slips his hand inside my leggings, making me grateful that I wore something comfortable—and conveniently more accessible.

"What if the driver sees?" I whisper.

"Then he'd catch us cuddling, taking in the view." He motions around us. "He'd be oblivious to the fact that my hand is buried inside your tight pussy."

Without warning, he shoves his hand into my panties, and I let out a soundless gasp as he plunges two long fingers inside me.

I clutch the blanket digging my nails into the fabric, willing myself to keep quiet.

"You're fucking drenched, baby." He lowers his mouth to my ear. "Have you been a naughty girl thinking about all the dirty things you want me to do to you?"

I nod rapidly as my wanton expression meets his.

Brooks gives me another scorching kiss, one so intense it feels like he's branding me as his.

He adds a third finger, pumping them in and out in measured strokes. My body coils tighter with each thrust, and when he finds my G-spot, I erupt, tumbling into orgasmic bliss. His mouth remains on mine, drowning out the sounds of my pleasure as I ride his hand.

I adjust the shower head to the high-pressure jet setting, and the water pulsates against my core.

My breath comes out in shallow gasps as the vivid scene plays out in my mind, and then another fantasy enters my thoughts, clear as day.

Brooks is in the shower, kneeling in front of me. His hands grip my thighs as he licks my pussy in long, steady strokes. A low groan passes my lips, and I wind my fingers in his hair to draw him closer as he sucks on my clit hard, igniting a fire inside me. He coaxes me to come using his tongue, and when he calls me his pretty girl, I soar into a state of ecstasy.

His heated gaze never leaves mine as he laps up the remnants of my pleasure.

When I've come back to my senses, he helps me stand and spins me around to face the wall.

I press my hands against the cool tile, hyper-aware of his hand on my hip, his fingers digging into my skin. His other hand guides his shaft inside me, causing me to whimper at the sensation of being so full. Once he's fully seated, he moves his hand to my breasts, teasing my nipples.

My hands remain in place, and when I tip my head back, I find his unbridled expression as he impales me with his cock at a punishing pace.

"Oh, god, Brooks, please don't stop," I moan, reaching down to strum my clit with my free hand.

My eyes fly open when I feel a subtle chill in the air, looking over to find him standing in the bathroom doorway. He's watching me with fire in his eyes, his gaze zoned in on my naked body.

Holy shit. He's real.

I yank my hand from between my thighs, and the showerhead goes slack in my other hand, the water splashing against the tiles below.

Despite the steam and my lust-filled haze, I notice his hand palming his hard-on. My cheeks flush as he peruses me with a piercing glance like he's proud of the effect he has on me.

The logical side of my brain insists I put a stop to this immediately and demand he leave, yet my visceral reaction is irrefutable. I'm wild with a hunger that I can't ignore and the desire to see his unfiltered reaction as I fall apart before him overrides the final thread of reason I'm holding on to.

The way he looks at me like I'm the only thing he wants, gives me the confidence to trail my hand down my chest and trace my nipples with my fingertip. I then slowly move down to my navel, pausing briefly before getting to my core. When I aim the showerhead back at my pussy, Brooks' jaw is clenched as he tugs down his sweats, taking out his rigid cock and strokes it. I gulp at the size, unsure how that could ever fit inside me.

If there's a will, there's a way, right?

I watch as he pumps himself faster, his hand gliding up and down his shaft in fluid movements.

"Show me how beautiful you are when you come," He groans.

Under the weight of his relentless gaze, I strum my clit with fervor. My chest heaves, and my lips part on a guttural cry as my orgasm hits me like a freight train. Brooks murmurs my name like a prayer as he follows me over the edge.

I slump against the shower wall as I come down from my euphoria.

When the lustful haze subsides, I look through the steamy glass into the steely eyes of the man who unraveled me.

Brooks keeps his gaze fixed on me as he heads to the sink and washes himself off. Once he's dried his cock, he tucks it back inside his boxers and pulls his pants back up.

"I just came back to grab my phone. I realized halfway to the gym that I forgot it, but *this*," he gestures toward me, "was a very pleasant surprise." He tosses his towel into the hamper in the corner. "You're going to be my ruin, Lila Monroe, and I'm not even sorry about it." He smirks before leaving the bathroom.

Heat blooms in my cheeks, my thoughts reeling from the unexpected turn of events. I should be embarrassed, but more than anything, I can't help but wish he had joined me in the shower to make my fantasies a reality.

After finishing my shower, I come out of the bathroom to find Winston sprawled out, batting his toy hippo across the floor without a care in the world.

"You couldn't have barked to warn me that Brooks was here? I thought you didn't like him," I playfully scold. "You better be careful, Winn. It's in your best interest to put a stop to whatever is happening between Brooks and me, or you might be resigned to sleeping in your dog bed indefinitely," I tease.

Although I'd never allow Winston to sleep in his own bed long-term, there is a part of me that likes the idea of Brooks sticking around. I know it's unrealistic since he has a career and has to get back to California after the wedding, but that doesn't stop me from daydreaming about what could be, no matter how impossible it sounds.

Bored of his toy, Winston plants himself by the entryway, pawing at the door. When I take too long, he shoots me a pointed look, urging me to hurry up.

"I'm coming," I promise, pulling on a hoodie and fleece-lined leggings.

He spins in a tight circle, letting out impatient yips while I put on my boots.

I'd be lying if I said I wasn't a little nervous about facing Brooks after what just occurred. I shake my head, wondering what in the world got into me. If any other man had walked in on me touching myself in the shower, I wouldn't have had the confidence to take a risk and act on my impulses.

Brooks is the exception.

I've always preferred to play it safe, seeking comfort in routine and stability, whether that's missionary position in the bedroom or the quiet of my small town. In the past, flirting with concepts like moving across the country or starting my own event planning business has been a safe space—a way to feel daring without stepping outside my comfort zone.

The more time I spend with Brooks, the less daunting the idea of taking risks becomes, and the more exhilarating it sounds. It's as if his presence has unlocked Pandora's box, revealing a side of me that I've kept locked away for so long.

Whether he heads back to the west coast after Christmas or we explore something deeper, one thing is certain; there's no returning to the safe, predictable version of myself.

When Winston and I get to the inn, I don't expect to find Kay pacing the lobby. She's muttering under her breath as she scrolls through her phone. For someone as calm and collected as she is, it's obvious something has rattled her.

Brooks stands nearby, leaning against the wall, arms crossed, with my mom and Hannah beside him, their concern evident.

I glance over at Brooks but quickly avert my gaze when I feel the heat rising to my cheeks.

"What's going on?" I ask, looking between them and Kay.

Hannah shakes her head. "We're not sure. When your mom and I got here, Kay was on the phone. She became agitated, and after she hung up, she started pacing, and she hasn't stopped long enough for us to find out what's wrong."

I tentatively approach Kay, resting my hand on her shoulder.

She stops pacing and looks up from her phone. "What is it, dear?" she asks, her voice tight.

"What's the matter?"

"Santa canceled," she replies with a defeated sigh. "David is under the weather and isn't able to make it tonight. I've reached out to several people, but no one else is available on such short notice."

"Oh, no. I'm sorry to hear that."

Every Christmas Eve, Kay hosts a special event at the inn where all the kids get to meet Santa and share their Christmas wishlist with him. It's been a tradition for as long as I can remember, and it's the highlight for so many families.

My mom used to bring Andrew and me when we were little, and back then, Brooks' dad dressed as Santa. After he passed, Kay hired David, Starlight Pines police chief, to carry on the tradition, but it looks like this year, we might not have a Santa at all. My parents have plans with my aunt and uncle, who are in town for the wedding, or I'm sure my dad would do it in a heartbeat.

The idea of letting down all the kids coming tonight crushes me.

Kay taps her fingers against her lips, her gaze flitting to Brooks, who's still standing silently by the wall, his face unreadable.

"I've got it," she exclaims, clapping her hands together with a grin. "Brooks, you'll be our Santa this year."

He blinks in surprise, his shoulders stiffening. "You want me to do what?"

"To play Santa," Kay repeats, her tone gentle but insistent.

"I'd rather not."

"Don't be such a grump," she teases. "The kids are really looking forward to it. You wouldn't want to let them down now, would you?"

"Grandma, I'd prefer to leave the costumes and holiday cheer to someone else."

"What happened to the boy who used to check his stocking every morning, the week before Christmas, hoping Santa came early? You used to love the holidays, just like your dad. That holiday spirit is still in you; it's merely waiting to be rediscovered."

"I appreciate your concern, but a guilt trip won't sway me," Brooks says.

My eyes widen when Kay drops her cell phone, and it crashes to the floor. She puts a hand on her heart and stumbles backward. Her face scrunches in pain as she falls into the chair behind her, closing her eyes and leaning to the side.

Brooks rushes over to her, and I'm not far behind.

"Kay," I shout, my voice rising in panic.

"Grandma. Are you okay?" Brooks says as he falls to his knees in front of her.

Kay places a hand on her chest. "Do you hear that," she asks, and we stop and listen. "It's the sound of my heart breaking. I could have another heart attack at any minute, and all I'll remember is that my grandson's last words to me were that he wouldn't be Santa for Christmas."

I cover my mouth with my hand, fighting back laughing at her antics. She's the only person I know who would use her condition to guilt trip someone into doing what she wants.

Brooks rises to his feet. "Seriously, Grandma?"

Kay cracks an eye open and looks up at him. "I'm beginning to think you're the real Grinch here, stealing Christmas from your poor old grandmother and the kids."

Brooks runs a hand across his face. "What's it going to take to guarantee you never do *this* again?" He motions to her dramatically slumped on the chair.

"Is that a yes to playing Santa?" Kay asks with a smirk. "Lila can assist. I've got an elf costume she can wear. It's going to be perfect." She sits up, clasping her hands together, her lips curling into an expectant smile as though she's already anticipating what his answer will be.

He lets out an exasperated sigh. "Fine, but only if Lila agrees to join me."

Wait. Join him for what?

My mouth falls open when it finally registers that Kay just volunteered me to play the part of the elf. The last thing Brooks and I need is to be in close proximity today. Not when the sexual tension between us is taut, stretched to its breaking point.

"Wait a minute," I say to Kay. "I can't be an elf. I promised Hannah we'd have our own bachelorette celebration tonight, complete with dinner, homemade cocktails, and a movie marathon since she didn't get to have one."

Maybe Brooks and I should hatch an escape plan together that doesn't involve Kay faking another medical emergency. Although, considering I'm actively avoiding eye contact with him right now, that complicates things.

"That's not important," Hannah interjects with a dismissive wave. "You have to do this. The kids need you more than I do tonight." She winks. "Andrew and I can manage our last night engaged with a cozy night in and some takeout."

How am I supposed to argue with that?

"Well?" Kay asks, her gaze bouncing between Brooks and me. "Is that a yes? Is Christmas Eve saved?"

Brooks' unreadable mask slips, looking at me with a smirk. "What do you say, Lila?"

I exhale dramatically, the corner of my mouth twitching upward. "I guess I don't have much of a choice, do I?"

He tilts his head slightly, his mouth fading into a smile, and suddenly playing the elf to his Santa sounds far more appealing than it should.

"This is perfect!" Kay exclaims. "I'll go get those costumes steamed so they're ready for tonight." She heads off in the direction of her room.

"Now that we have that settled, there's something your mom and I want to show you," Hannah chimes in.

"Okay." I nod.

I give Brooks one last fleeting glance before following Hannah and my mom into Kay's office, where there's a white garment bag hanging from the coat rack in the corner.

I gasp, turning to Hannah. "Is this your wedding dress?"

She stumbled upon her dream dress at Starlight Pines' only bridal boutique earlier this week, and luckily the staff was able to handle the minor alterations on short notice. She and my mom picked it up this morning and must have come straight to the inn afterward.

I'm confused when Hannah shakes her head. "No. This one is for you." She motions to the bag. "Why don't you look inside."

My fingers tremble as I pull the zipper down to reveal a stunning red gown with a sweetheart neckline and intricate sequin detailing.

I gape at her in disbelief. "This doesn't match your color scheme."

I had planned on wearing a simple dark blue dress that I already owned. There's an unspoken rule about never outshining the bride, and I can't help but worry this gown would cross that line. Especially since it's not her wedding colors.

Hannah gives my shoulder a squeeze. "You're my maid of honor and deserve to wear a dress as stunning as this one. Your mom's dress is also red, and it'll look great with the guys' silver ties. It's my wedding day, and this is what I want you to wear," she adds when I hesitate.

"Wait until you put it on. It was made for you," my mom chimes in, giving my arm a light squeeze.

Tears well up in my eyes as I give them both hugs. "Thank you. I can't wait to wear it."

The holidays have a special way of bringing people together, and it's one of the reasons I love them so much. And while Christmas weddings are my favorite, this one is extra special since I've had the opportunity to help Hannah create the winter wonderland she envisioned for her big day. I can only hope that someday I'll be celebrating my own winter wedding at the inn.

CHAPTER 10

L ATER THAT NIGHT I PEEK AROUND THE CORNER INTO THE lobby with a frown on my face. Grandma insisted that I wear the full Santa costume, including the itchy beard, extra padding around my middle, and boots that pinch my toes. I'm having shit luck this week when it comes to getting stuck in situations where I'm forced to wear ill-fitted footwear. At least tonight I'm indoors and not chasing a stubborn dachshund through the snow.

The lobby is buzzing with guests who've come to meet Santa. I spot Winston in a festive red sweater covered in white snowflakes, trailing after a group of kids and eagerly cleaning up the crumbs from their gingerbread cookies.

Grandma is at the reception desk, and when she notices me, she stops midway through filling a bowl with candy canes to come and give me a hug.

"Brooks, you look just like your father." Her voice cracks as she wipes away a tear.

Before his passing, my dad always donned the red suit and loved meeting with all the town kids. I swear I can hear his hearty laugh, the kind that filled the room and made everything seem a little brighter.

I swallow hard as Grandma pulls me into a hug. A week ago, I would have torn this suit off or walked out the door the second she compared to my dad. Christmas has always been a reminder of losing him, and I've been avoiding all our traditions because I couldn't face them without him.

This year feels different.

My attention shifts to Lila, who just walked inside dressed in a green elf costume, complete with candy cane striped tights and curled-toe shoes.

Her blonde hair is pulled into a loose braid down her back, leaving a few strands to frame her face—the flush enhancing her cheekbones and the vivid blue of her eyes. There's a spark of amusement in her expression, making her look almost ethereal.

"Lila's beautiful, isn't she," Grandma says from beside me.

"Yeah," I reply, my voice almost a whisper.

She nudges me with a knowing smile. "You better hurry up. The kids are waiting."

I avert my gaze, swallowing hard. "Right, the kids," I grumble.

When I step into the lobby, all eyes are on me. Several kids shuffle closer, clutching their handwritten lists tightly. As I'm taking a deep breath, trying to shake off the nerves, Lila appears at my side, her hand slipping into mine for a brief squeeze.

"I'm glad you're here, *Santa*. You're going to do great," she hums.

Her encouragement pushes me forward, and I stride toward the oversized red velvet chair with gold trim that I helped Grandma set up near the fireplace this afternoon. Once seated, I flash the kids a smile and let out a hearty "Ho, ho, ho! Merry Christmas!"

They erupt in cheers as Lila and my grandma direct them to form a line. The first kid in front is a little girl holding a stuffed reindeer. She tugs on its frayed ear, her wide eyes peeking out from beneath her bangs. I watch as she takes a tentative step toward me, then hesitates.

Before she can bolt, Lila crouches down next to her and brushes the hair from her face. "Don't be scared, sweetie. Santa is really nice." The little girl gives me another once-over before giving Lila a skeptical look.

"Can you go first?" she asks Lila, her voice wary.

Lila glances between us, a slight blush creeping onto her cheeks. After briefly hesitating, she leans down, giving the girl a warm smile and squeezing her hand.

"Sure, sweetie. I'd be happy to," she says.

My mind blanks when Lila rises and walks toward me. She perches on my knee, looping her arm around my neck for support. I place my hand on her back, and when her fingers brush the nape of my neck, it sends a jolt down my spine.

She tilts her head, those crystal-blue eyes meeting mine, leaving me defenseless against the heat of her touch.

Lila schools her expression, grinning down at the little girl who's watching us closely. "See, Santa isn't so bad. Ready for your turn now?" she asks, sliding off my lap.

The little girl inches closer, clutching her reindeer to her chest. With a tiny nod, she bravely steps forward, glancing back at Lila for reassurance before letting me lift her onto my knee. Her legs dangle, and a ghost of a smile crosses her lips when I lean in and ask, "What's your name, little one?"

She tilts her chin up and declares, "Penny, and I'm not little. I'm six."

I chuckle softly. "Six, huh? You're right; that's definitely not little. Any ideas of what you want for Christmas this year?" I ask, adjusting her on my knee.

Penny's eyes light up as she launches into a detailed

description of a blue dollhouse with a kitchen stocked with pretend food, a porch swing, and a tiny mailbox that opens and closes.

When she finally stops to catch her breath, I lean in and whisper, "I think the elves are going to have a blast making that for you. Don't you think so?" I ask Lila, who's standing nearby holding a bowl of candy canes.

She beams down at Penny. "Absolutely. Just so long as Santa remembers to double-check his naughty and nice list," she says, giving me a wink.

"I pick up all my toys when Mommy asks, so I'm definitely on the nice list," Penny says, puffing her chest out with pride. "And I always eat my vegetables, except for those little green balls." She scrunches her nose and sticks out her tongue.

I chuckle. "Peas?"

She shakes her head. "No. Peas are my favorite."

"Do you mean Brussel sprouts?"

"Yeah. Those." She makes a face like she ate something sour. "Those are gross. I tried feeding them to a dog once and even *he* didn't eat them."

I lean in and whisper in her ear. "I have a secret for you, kid. I don't like Brussel sprouts either." She giggles into her hands as I lean back and declare, "Don't worry, Santa doesn't care if you don't like them. You're a shoo-in for the nice list."

She claps her hands. "Did you hear that Mommy? I'm a shoo-in," she exclaims to a woman standing nearby, her brown eyes lighting up at the sight of her daughter's enthusiasm. They have the same jet-black hair, contrasting with their pale skin.

"Of course you are, Penn," her mom says.

She comes over to help her off my lap.

"Thanks for your patience," she tells me and Lila.

"It was no trouble," Lila grins. "Merry Christmas, Penny."

"Merry Christmas," she shouts back as her mom tugs her toward the exit.

That's when I notice the threadbare patches at the elbows of Penny's sweater and the worn cuffs of her jeans. It makes me wonder if money is tight for her family and if Santa will be able to visit her this year.

God, I hope so.

My dad's old charity, The Holiday Claus Foundation, comes to mind. Its mission was to ensure that the kids in Starlight Pines and the surrounding areas had presents under the tree, regardless of their parents' financial situation. It was a family affair—my dad handled fundraising and identified those who needed help most, my brothers and I picked out most of the toys, and my grandma would wrap them.

When he passed, I shoved the charity to the furthest corner of my mind, thinking someone else in the community would step up to carry it forward. Now, I'm wondering if I was wrong to assume that.

The last thing I want is for Penny or the other kids to go without.

By the time we've gotten through the long line of kids eager for their turn with Santa, I'm so ready for it to be over. One boy nearly yanking my beard off, and a three-year-old demanded a pony with a purple tail. Glad I'm not the one who has to explain why there isn't one waiting under her tree come morning.

Although I was hesitant at first, I can't deny playing Santa turned out better than expected. Surprisingly, it helped me feel closer to my dad than I have in a long time, making me wonder if the best way to keep his memory alive is to celebrate the holiday that he loved the most.

My shift in perspective is all thanks to Lila. She's taught me how to find joy in the little things, and now I'm beginning to believe that maybe, just maybe, it's possible to learn to be happy again.

Having her by my side tonight made all the difference—she

has a way with kids that's enchanting. They might have come to see Santa, but it was her voice and infectious smile that had them hanging on her every word. She brought a special kind of wonder to the event, and I'm grateful I could be a part of it.

The real magic of Christmas isn't the presents wrapped in ribbon or the light-covered trees—it's her.

I have my grandma to thank for bringing us together tonight. Her persistence may be overwhelming at times, but she usually knows best.

Once I've ditched the itchy beard, I take a sip of water from the bottle Lila brought me earlier. I scan the room, checking to see if she's back from helping a single mom get her kids into the car.

She's across the room, leaning against the reception desk, talking to a guy in a baggy flannel and beanie. His back is facing me so I can't see his face, but there's something very familiar about him.

I assume he's a guest staying at the inn until he gives her arm a familiar squeeze. He says something that causes her to laugh, and the musical sound is like a magnet, drawing me closer.

Who the hell is that?

It's evident they know each other, but I don't appreciate how friendly he is with Lila. She might not officially be mine, but after what happened between us this morning, I was looking forward to exploring whatever this thing is between us.

A red haze clouds my vision, and my jaw ticks as I watch the stranger lean in to hug her. My patience snaps when I catch the smile on Lila's face, the one she reserves for people she's close with. Before I can stop myself, I march over.

"Who's your friend?" I ask, disregarding her questioning stare as I pull her to my side, wrapping an arm around her waist.

"We all know you like being the center of attention, but that outfit is next-level, Brooks," a familiar voice drawls.

My jaw drops when I look up to find my brother is the mystery man. "Jameson?"

When we video chat, he's always wearing his white coat or a button-up shirt with tailored pants and polished dress shoes. He's hardly recognizable in a flannel jacket, boot cut jeans, and boots. Plus, the beanie hides his black hair, typically trimmed short in a crew cut.

He mentioned arriving on Christmas Eve, but he hasn't called me since I arrived in town, so I wasn't sure if he'd follow through. He practically lives at the hospital and rarely takes a day off, even during the holidays. Something we have in common.

"He came to visit your grandma, too. Isn't that nice?" Lila interjects with a smile.

"Yeah, very nice," I say as I tug her closer.

Jameson throws his head back and laughs. "You didn't tell me you were dating Lila Monroe, brother."

I glower at him but don't get a chance to respond before Grandma spots him.

"Jameson? Is that really you?" She hurries over to my brother, squeezing his cheeks affectionately before drawing him in for a hug. "Would it hurt for you boys to give me a heads up that you're coming? Is Calder with you?" She glances over his shoulder.

Jameson shakes his head. "Sorry, Grandma. He's still in Nepal without cell service."

Her eyes betray a hint of sadness before she conceals it. "Well, I'm glad you and Brooks made it." She gives his cheek another pat. "How long are you here for?"

He rakes a hand through his hair. "That's actually something I want to talk to you about."

"Sounds ominous," Grandma chuckles. "Let's save this conversation for after Christmas. We've got a wedding to celebrate, and I want to soak up every minute with my grandsons while I can." She reaches out and holds both our hands.

Another pang of guilt strikes me when I consider how diffi-cult it must have been for her that we've stayed away for so long. It's hard to imagine the void she must've felt.

Being back in Starlight Pines has made me realize how fleet-ing time is, and I don't want to miss any more moments with my family then I already have. They should always come first, and I only wish it hadn't taken me this long to realize that. I thought I was protecting myself by staying away, but I've only been running from what matters most.

"Hope you like sleeping in the storage room," I tell Jameson with a smirk.

Since the cot broke, I guess he'll have to settle for a make-shift bed of blankets. Now that he's a big-wig doctor, he prefers the finer things in life, like private jets, tailored suits, and five-star hotels. Needless to say, I'm going to get a kick out of him rough-ing it for a few days.

Grandma pats Jameson on the arm. "Nonsense," she tells him. "You can sleep on one of the other foldable beds. There's plenty of space for one in my room."

I stare at her, certain I must have heard her wrong. "I'm sorry, the *what* now?"

Lila puts her hand on my chest, chiming in. "We have several fold-out beds on hand for when guests need additional sleeping arrangements."

"Is there a particular reason I wasn't offered one of those, Grandma?"

She shrugs. "We have a full house, and I assumed they were all in use. It wasn't until yesterday, when I checked the spare linen closet that I realized we had a couple still available."

Bullshit.

She's the most organized person I know—there's no way she overlooked something like this. Come to think of it, when I tried asking her about a replacement, she deflected.

"It's getting late, and we all have a big day ahead of us," she announces. "I'm going to get Jameson's bed set up, and then Winn and I have a date with a holiday rom-com and some peanut butter biscuits." Winston, who's been resting in a dog bed near the front desk, perks up at the mention of treats and trots over to my grandma, pressing his nose against her leg, demanding she follow up on her promise.

He might be a bossy little thing, but I admit, he's starting to grow on me.

"You don't have to take Winn tonight," Lila interjects. "I'll make sure he gets a treat."

"Hush now," Grandma says with her hands on her hips. "He's staying with me, and that's final. We'll see you two in the morning." She bends down to scoop Winston into her arms and heads toward her room. "Come along, Jameson," she calls over her shoulder.

"Looks like I'm being summoned," he says with a hint of amusement in his tone. "It was nice to see you, Lila." He gives her arm an affectionate squeeze, earning a sharp look from me. "I'll leave you two to it," he adds with a knowing grin as he follows Grandma out of the room.

Lila and I are left alone, the silence lingering in the air.

My mind drifts back to the unexpected surprise waiting for me after I finished my workout this morning. The last thing I expected was to come back to the cottage to the sound of moans coming from the bathroom. Curiosity got the best of me, and I froze in place when I found Lila in the shower with the showerhead between her legs, my name passing her lips while she stroked her clit with one hand and the showerhead in the other.

It's only been three days.

Three days of stolen glances, every touch leaving me wanting more, and a chemistry so electric, it's felt like I'm on the brink of something monumental.

Our kiss in the photo booth sealed my fate, setting off a

chain of events I wasn't prepared for. Her beauty is mesmerizing, her wit intoxicating, and the way she makes my body burn is all-consuming.

I tried staying away, but after witnessing her unravel before my eyes, I'm done resisting.

I want this woman.

No, I *need* this woman, and I can't wait another minute to claim her.

"Ready to go back to the cottage?" Lila asks, her voice breathless. "Unless you'd prefer to sleep on one of those fold-out beds tonight," she teases.

I place my hand on the small of her back, gripping her hip with the other hand. "Let's go back to your place," I whisper in her ear.

CHAPTER 11

I CLOSE THE DOOR BEHIND US, RESTING MY PALM AGAINST the frame as I take a steadying breath.

"Can we do that every year? It was so much fun." Lila beams, shrugging off her coat and hanging it on the rack in the corner. "The kids' faces were priceless when they sat on your lap. It's adorable that they were convinced we're from the North Pole. Kay definitely deserves a thank you for talking us into doing it."

I'm having trouble concentrating with the stray piece of hair falling against her cheek and the way her eyes dance with excitement as she speaks.

"I still can't believe she forgot about those extra fold-out beds. Usually, they're all in use, so it didn't cross my mind to ask if any were available. On the bright side, Jameson won't have to sleep on the floor tonight." She chuckles.

My jaw tightens as I watch her kick off her boots, her laugh making the pressure in my chest almost unbearable.

Lila glances at me, a crease forming between her brows. "Brooks, are you okay?"

Her cheeks are still tinged with color, and her concern for me is my undoing.

"Fuck it," I say under my breath.

I stride toward her, my pulse thundering in my ears, knowing there's no turning back now.

She takes a step back, bumping up against the closest wall. I press my hands against either side of her head, trapping her in. Her chest heaves as her breaths come out in short, uneven gasps.

"Brooks, what are you—"

"I've wanted to do this all night," I say, cutting her off.

She remains perfectly still as I raise my hand, and with delicate precision, I trace her angelic face, my fingers trailing across her forehead, moving to her right cheekbone and then her left. My exploration continues, gliding across her freckled nose and running the pad of my thumb across her mouth. I let out a low growl when she parts her lips and nips the tip of my thumb.

"God, what are you doing to me," I murmur. "I haven't been able to concentrate all day."

"And why might that be?" she asks with a sly smirk.

"I can't get the images of your perfect body out of my head." I pause briefly, leaning down so my mouth brushes against hers, her chest heaving. "While I was jerking off, I imagined what you'd taste like while my face is buried in your pretty pussy." She gasps at my declaration. "Want to know something else? Seeing you with Jameson tonight made me jealous."

She raises a brow, amused. "It did?"

"Hell, yes. Observing another man touch you after watching you come with *my* name on your lips was maddening." My fingers graze her cheek before sliding down to cup her jaw. "Do you have any idea how much power you have over me, baby?" I murmur in her ear. "You occupy every corner of my mind, and I want to taste and know every inch of your body. Kissing you was just an appetizer, and I'm starving for more." I nuzzle my nose into the crook of her neck, inhaling her delicious scent.

There's no question that I'd be disappointed if she denied

me, but I'd never push her into doing something she's not ready for, even if it means living with a perpetual hard-on for the foreseeable future.

She leans in closer, tracing a finger down my chest. "I haven't been able to stop thinking about what happened during my shower this morning either." She exhales deeply, a glint of challenge flashing in her eyes. "Why don't you show me all the things you want to do to me, Brooks? Don't make me wait any longer."

Her words make me want to strip her bare in an instant, but her gaze holds me in place, making me want to slow down and relish every second of this.

The heat builds in my veins as I trace her collarbone and push her hair over her shoulder, revealing the soft curve of her neck. I place one hand on her waist and slowly turn her around before I use my other hand to drag down the zipper of her dress. When I'm finished, I ease one sleeve off her shoulder, then the other. Her dress falls to the ground. Lila steps out of it, and I suppress a groan when she turns back around to face me, giving me an unfiltered view of her revealing lace lingerie—a red-laced bra paired with a matching lace thong.

Hot damn.

"Did you wear this for me, pretty girl?"

Red is officially my favorite color.

She nods, her cheeks flushed. "Do you like it?"

"Like it? I fucking love it." I slowly trace the cups of the bra, admiring the delicate lace against her fair skin.

Her eyes stay glued to mine as I lean forward to kiss the swells of her breasts and tug down the straps from her shoulders. With expert precision, I wind my hands around her and unclasp her bra. It flutters to the ground, giving me an unfiltered view of her rosy nipples. They're begging for my attention, but I restrain myself for a little while longer.

Lila's breath catches when I lift her into my arms and carry her to the bed. I gently lay her down in the middle and move back to take in the view.

"You're a goddamn vision," I growl.

I'm captivated by her hourglass figure and sinful curves. Her body is a work of art, and I have the privilege to experience it first-hand. I'm damned lucky she's all mine.

At least for tonight.

There's no telling what tomorrow might bring, so I plan to savor every precious moment I have with her—starting now.

I bend to kiss the valley between her full, round breasts, and she draws in a sharp breath when I flick one of her nipples with my tongue. The small, deep pink bud hardens at my touch, and I greedily wrap my mouth around it, biting down on the soft flesh as she mewls.

"You like that?" I murmur against her breast. "Thinking about what my tongue would feel like licking that pretty pussy of yours?"

"Oh, god, yes," she cries out.

Lila puts her hands on my shoulders, her nails sinking into my bare flesh, and I welcome the pain. Her moans grow louder as I alternate between licking, biting, and sucking her sensitive breasts. She clings to me, and I fucking love every second.

With a light nudge to her hip, she lifts them up, allowing me to grab hold of the waistband of her thigh-high tights and tug them down. She lets out a sharp exhale when I trace her thighs with my fingers in lazy circles. I can smell the scent of her arousal, and when I get to her lace panties, I slowly drag them down her legs, one agonizing inch at a time. Lila keeps her hands on my shoulders, lifting one leg at a time so I can discard her clothes, tossing them to the floor. I place a tender kiss on her calf, glancing down to see her pussy already wet for me.

I shoot her a wicked grin as I swipe a finger along her seam. "Damn, baby, you're soaked." I drag my tongue along the column of her neck, peppering kisses across her collarbone.

Her gasp fills the room when I sink two fingers inside her tight heat, and she rocks into my hand seeking more friction.

"You're a needy thing, aren't you?"

She nods, biting her lip.

I thrust my fingers deeper inside, and she lets out a strangled cry. It's the most sensual sound I've ever heard, making me want her—want *this*—even more, if that's possible. Every second of waiting and longing has led to this moment, making our connection even more electric.

"Are you going to come on my hand?" I whisper, my heated gaze never leaving hers.

She clenches tighter around my hand. "Please don't stop," she breathes out.

"Not until you come for me."

I can sense that she's close to losing control, her body coiling tighter with each plunge of my fingers. I thrum her clit with my thumb, and within seconds, she shatters around my hand.

Her head falls back on the pillow as she lets out a strangled cry, plummeting off the precipice. She doesn't stop riding my hand until I've wrung every drop of desire from her core.

Lila is wholly mesmerizing when she's on the verge of release, but watching her come undone in pure bliss is beyond anything I imagined.

"Taste yourself." I lift my fingers to her lips.

Her eyes grow dilated as her tongue darts out and she hums with satisfaction as she swirls it around the tips.

When she's finished, I flash her a playful smile and bring my fingers to my mouth groaning as I suck them clean, relishing the taste of her on my tongue. "Delicious."

"Brooks, I want you inside me," she murmurs. "Now."

I pause at her plea. Hell, I'd be lying if I said having sex with her hadn't crossed my mind, but it isn't on the agenda for tonight, or I would have come better prepared.

"I don't have a condom."

"I'm on the pill, and I'm clean," she rushes out, her eyes aflame with lust.

"I haven't been with anyone since I was tested months ago, and I always wear a condom." *Until now.* "Are you sure you want this? Because once I'm inside you, I won't be able to stop," I say in warning.

She cups my jaw, grazing my cheek with her thumb. "Who says I want you to hold back?"

Her invitation has me off the bed in record time, stripping out of my clothes and leaving them in a haphazard pile on the floor.

Once I'm back on the bed hovering above Lila, I grab hold of my shaft and line myself up with her entrance. I run the tip of my dick along her seam in teasing strokes, coating myself with her wetness. Damn, I'm not even inside her yet and I'm already finding it hard to control myself. I push inside slowly, and her pussy clenches around me at the intrusion. She threads her fingers through my hair, tugging me closer as our intermingled groans fill the room.

"Oh my god," she gasps when I pull out then push back in deeper.

I kiss her forehead. "Relax for me, baby. I'm not all the way in yet."

She bites her lip, her expression clouded with uncertainty.

"Don't worry, pretty girl—it'll fit."

After I smooth her hair away from her face, I move my hand to the nape of her neck and graze my thumb along her jaw. Tilting her chin up, I claim her mouth with mine, savoring her soft sighs.

I ease the rest of the way in, and once I'm fully seated, I pause to give her a moment to adjust. She's still a little tense, so I massage her clit with my thumb, and within seconds she relaxes below me.

"You're so goddamn tight," I grit out, my voice strained.

"Move. I need you to move," she pleads.

I intertwine our fingers, guiding her arms above her head,

and begin moving in a steady rhythm. Lila meets me thrust for thrust, and I embrace the warmth as she welcomes me into her pussy. The very idea of saying goodbye to her leaves a hollow pit in my stomach, but I quickly shove it aside, determined to focus on the here and now with her splayed out to worship and cherish.

I brush my tongue against her lips before slipping it inside her mouth. She moans loudly as I pick up my pace and shift the angle of my cock to press against her G-spot.

"You feel *so* good," Lila pants out, writhing beneath me, desperate for release.

"Are you going to come for me again?"

"Holy shit," she cries. Her desire for me is magnetic, especially when she's on the cusp of an electrifying orgasm. "Please, Brooks, I need you."

Her unfiltered honesty stirs something deep inside as I pound into her without restraint. All rational thought is gone as the primal sound of skin slapping against skin resonates in the air. She flies higher into a state of euphoria, digging her fingernails into my palms. She looks up at me with her captivating blue eyes, filled with lust and silently begging me for more.

Unable to resist her a minute longer, I reach one hand down and pinch her clit, sending her into freefall. I roar as unfiltered pleasure surges through me at the beautiful sight of her falling apart before my eyes. I hold her tight as we ride out our orgasms together.

"Fuck, you're so perfect, coming around my dick." I nuzzle my nose into her neck, inhaling the sweet scent of peppermint.

I carefully pull out of her, not wanting to cause her pain, and I stifle another groan as I watch our mixed cum drip down her thigh.

What is this woman doing to me?

I lower myself beside her, wrapping an arm around her waist. She instinctively curls into me, resting her head on my chest.

When she gives me a sated smile, I can't resist running a hand through her hair, the strands falling through my fingers like silk.

"Sex with you is beyond anything I've imagined, but I've recently discovered I'm a big fan of cuddling with you too," Lila says as she runs a hand along my stomach.

"Good thing we're on the same page then," I say with a smirk.

I guide her face toward mine and capture her mouth. Her swollen lips are soft against mine, and the kiss is tender. Her breath is warm against my face, and with my free hand, I trace the curve of her jaw, committing it to memory. Our kiss deepens as she slides her tongue inside my mouth, slow and unhurried.

"Don't worry," I murmur against her lips. "We have all night to explore each other. I intend to learn the rhythm of your body, and become familiar with your reaction to every touch, before the sun rises."

"Brooks." She places her hand firmly on my chest. "Promise me one thing. Can we wait to talk about what happens next until after the wedding?" She glances down at the bed. "Tonight is more than I could have ever asked for, and I don't want to spoil it."

Lila's right. There's no telling what tomorrow will bring. I'm supposed to go back to California after the wedding, but I can't help to second-guess myself.

I look down at her, the tension wrung from her body, a thin sheen of sweat covering her breasts. My heart is still racing after what just felt like an out-of-body experience. Now that I've had sex with her once, I have every intention of doing it again if she'll let me.

We've crossed the point of no return, and yet I wouldn't change a thing. The only way forward is with Lila. The future is full of possibilities, and I can't imagine facing it with anyone but her.

For now, I'm content having her in my arms, confident that when the time is right, I'll tell her how much she means to me.

"Sure." I press a kiss to her forehead. "Just know that we're not stopping until we're both boneless."

She giggles. "Mmm, I like the sound of that." She leans forward to kiss me again.

Lila's radiant smile leaves me to wonder what it would be like to wake up to that sight every morning and go to bed with it every night. I'm willing to do anything to make that happen.

CHAPTER 12

Lila

WHEN I WAKE UP, BROOKS IS STILL ASLEEP. IN PLACE OF his usual frown lines, his features are smoothed, and he appears relaxed in a way I've barely seen all week.

It's surreal to acknowledge that what's happening with Brooks isn't in my head. It's real, unrefined, and tangible. There's no need for grand gestures or dramatic declarations to understand our connection is special. With him, everything makes sense, and being in his arms last night felt like I might have found someone who could be *my* person. The one who I can build a life with, where every small moment means something special, and who reminds me daily that I'm his one and only.

My only regret is putting off the conversation about what comes next. What if he wakes up and decides what we've shared is nothing more than a fleeting mistake? It's an irrational thought, but the uncertainty is difficult to ignore.

It's the morning of the wedding, and the responsible thing to do would be to get ready and start final prep, but I'm tempted to stay in bed and savor having this handsome man in my bed a little while longer.

I pull back the covers, giving me an unobstructed view of

Brooks. He's sexy as hell, and when I notice his hard-on, I move down to where his cock is jutting out, demanding attention. I tentatively lean forward and run my finger along the thick shaft, watching it twitch at the sensation.

Unable to resist, I place a hand on his hip and wrap my hand around his heated erection, hovering my mouth over the head and glide my tongue across the crown.

Brooks stirs, groaning as he peeks an eye open. "Morning, beautiful."

"Good morning," I hum, licking him again.

He lets out a low groan, and I lift my hooded eyes to meet his smoldering gaze as I curl my fingers tighter around his cock. He takes a sharp intake of breath as I move my hand up and down his shaft in slow, steady strokes. Pre-cum leaks from the tip, and I lean down to lap it up with my tongue.

"Damn, baby, I could get used to waking up like this," he says, tone dripping with desire.

My hands glide along his inner thighs, tracing the contours of his impressive physique as I continue to worship his cock.

He props himself up on his elbow so he has a better view and winds his fingers through my hair, urging me to take him in my mouth. I eagerly suck the crown with fervor, and when he tightens his grip, coaxing me to take him deeper, I hollow my cheeks until his tip is at the back of my throat.

"Just like that," he croons, stroking the column of my neck, and letting me set the pace as I adjust.

I hum at hearing his praise, cupping his balls and squeezing gently as I suck him off. He loses all control, tugging my head forward, fucking my mouth with abandon as he lets out a low growl of approval. I'm drunk on the knowledge that I'm the reason for his unrestrained reaction.

"Fuck, I'm going to come," he groans.

His cock jerks in my hand as his cum fills my mouth. His

eyes widen as I lap up every drop, licking him clean. When I'm finished, his cock springs free from my mouth with a loud pop.

I squeal when he hoists me up the bed and flips me over onto my back.

"My turn." He grins wickedly.

He brushes his hand down my legs, leaving a trail of goosebumps in his wake. I wait with bated breath as he peppers kisses on my stomach. His stubble rubs against my skin as he moves toward my core, inch by torturous inch. My legs tremble with anticipation as he reaches the apex of my thighs.

He licks along the seam of my pussy before plunging his tongue inside. I buck my hips, grinding against his face as I grip his hair in my fists. He eagerly explores, alternating between licking and sucking, and when he thrusts two thick fingers inside me, a tantalizing shiver courses through my veins.

I gasp at the heat rippling through my body when I lift my head to see him buried between my legs.

I'm already wound tight from having my mouth on his cock, and right when I'm ready to fall apart he eases his pace, moving his fingers in and out in agonizingly slow strokes. My body coils tighter, frantic for him to move faster, and I cry out when he slows down even further.

"Brooks, please," I whimper, tugging his head closer.

He chuckles softly. "Haven't you heard that good things come to those who wait?" He teases, nipping the inside of my thigh. "Now keep those pretty eyes on me."

I release an exasperated breath but oblige, my gaze trained on him, unable to look away despite the rising tension building inside me.

He returns to teasing me with his fingers, and despite my silent pleas, he continues to draw out my impending orgasm.

Just when I think I can't take it anymore, he latches his mouth onto my clit, causing me to arch off the bed as a wave of euphoria crashes over me. My head drops back against the mattress as I call out his name, savoring every delicious second.

Once I come back down to earth, Brooks moves to the top of the bed and adjusts the pillows against the headboard. He gathers me into his arms and settles me comfortably on his chest as he leans back.

"Merry Christmas, Lila," he says, showering my shoulder with kisses.

"Merry Christmas, Brooks," I reply, my voice husky.

We stay like that for a while, looking into each other's eyes—two people caught in a shared moment that feels like it's changed everything.

Brooks finally glances over at the clock on the nightstand to see that it's 7:15 a.m. "What time do you need to be at the inn?" he asks.

My fingers wander across his chest, drawing aimless shapes. "The ceremony is at two, and Hannah is coming by the cottage to get ready at eleven. Although I should head over soon for a final walkthrough of the events room and to be ready for the vendors when they start arriving."

"What can I do to help? Put me to work, *boss*."

"You're at my service, huh? I like the sound of that," I say, tilting my head up to kiss him. "I could go for a cup of coffee. It's going to be a long day."

"I'll make sure you get your coffee, breakfast, *and at least one more orgasm*," he promises with a lazy smile.

"Not sure if we have time for the latter," I tease, pausing briefly to inhale his masculine scent. "I think I might be dreaming," I add hesitantly.

Brooks furrows his brow when he notices my shift in mood. "Why would you think that?"

I'm scared to say it out loud—that I don't want this to end. I've imagined this moment for so long, but now that it's real,

I'm terrified it'll slip away. What if, when Brooks goes back to California, he decides he's done with me, leaving me to pick up the pieces of my broken heart?

Last night exceeded anything I could have wished for, and I prefer to bask in blissful ignorance for as long as I can, clinging to the faint hope that he might feel a fraction of what I do.

I stick with the simple answer. "Because last night was incredible."

"*Just* last night, huh? Guess I didn't bring my A-game this morning." He winks. A beat passes before he straightens up, his expression turning serious. "Can I ask you something?"

"Of course," I reply.

My mind races with the possibilities of what it could be.

"If it weren't for my grandma relying on you to help at the inn, would you travel more?"

That's a good question.

"I'd like to think so. Only one other person knows this, but I've been thinking about moving away for a while, but it's never felt like the right time." I shift slightly, letting out a soft sigh. "And if I'm being honest, it's a scary concept."

He furrows his brow. "Why is that?"

"I've only ever worked at Whispering Pines," I admit, tucking a stray piece of hair behind my ear. "I started with Kay shortly after high school. It's the best job, and I've enjoyed every minute of it. But after most of my friends moved away, and I've spent time with brides from around the world, it made me question if I've only stayed because it's my safe space." I clear my throat before continuing. "I've considered moving to New York, where Fallon, my best friend lives, or to California to be closer to Andrew and Hannah. But if I did, that means I'd have to start over." A hint of vulnerability tinges my voice.

"The thing is, I love what I do, but event planners are a dime a dozen in big cities, and I'm not sure I'm cut out for that."

My eyes flutter when Brooks kisses my forehead. "You don't see it, do you?" he says softly. "I've attended my fair share of up-scale events, but what you've done with this wedding—especially on such short notice—is nothing short of remarkable. Hell, even the engagement party you put together was unlike any function I've attended. It was beyond impressive. With a portfolio like yours, you'd have clients lining up no matter where you go. You're that good."

I blink a couple of times, trying to steady myself as my belly does a flip. If Kay or my family had said that, I might have brushed it off, but Brooks doesn't say something unless he means it.

His encouraging words have chipped away at the last of my resolve, and no matter how hard I try to convince myself that I'm not falling for him, the truth is that I want this—I want *him*. And for more than the single night that we've shared.

"Thank you, Brooks," I say, stroking his stubbled cheek.

"I mean it," he states. "There's nothing more I'd like than to—"

My phone buzzes on the nightstand, cutting him off mid-sentence. He leans across to pick it up and hands it to me, a frown on his face. I'm not the only one who's unhappy that we were interrupted.

"Thanks," I tell him before picking it up.

"Hello, this is Lila," I answer.

"Good morning, dear," Kay says, sounding extra chipper this morning. "There are two people here from Pastry Haven with the wedding cake, and I wasn't sure how you wanted it set up."

I run a hand across my face as I switch to wedding planning mode. "They're early," I say as I scramble out of bed and yank open the top draw of my dresser. "They must have wanted to get this delivery out of the way so they could spend the rest of Christmas with their families." I rush to tug on a clean pair of underwear and fleece-lined leggings. "I'll be right there."

"I'm fixing them a cup of coffee, so you've got a few extra minutes," Kay says, accompanied by the clicking of glassware.

"Thanks, Kay. See you soon."

I'm pulling a sweater over my head when Brooks clears his throat. "Everything okay?"

"The wedding cake was delivered early, so I've got to meet with the bakers and get it set up."

Wordlessly, Brooks pushes the covers off and climbs out of bed. He's stark naked as he strides toward me. Every ripple and curvature of his well-defined abs are on display, and his cock juts out proudly as he saunters toward me.

My gaze is glued to him as he cups my cheek with his hands and moves his mouth to mine. When his tongue passes my lips, he grabs my jaw with his hands, deepening our kiss. I momentarily forget why I was in such a rush as we remain wrapped in our own private bubble.

When he finally pulls back, he rests his forehead against mine. "Fuck, you're going to be my undoing, beautiful." His fingers trace the bridge of my nose like he's committing every detail to memory. "You better get going. Kay and the vendor are waiting for you, remember?"

"Right," I say, taking a step back and rushing to put on my boots.

I have my hand on the door when Brooks calls my name.

"Yeah?" I ask, looking over my shoulder.

"Just to be clear. We're not done. Not by a long shot. I still owe you an orgasm, and I'm nothing if not a man of my word."

Heat rises to my cheeks, but my phone rings before I can respond.

Not again.

"Go." Brooks motions for the door. "There will be plenty of time for us to talk later. I promise."

I nod before ducking outside. Even as the cold air hits me,

I can still feel the heat of his gaze. Despite my lingering doubts about what comes next, his words echo in my mind, and I allow the hope stirring inside me to take root.

Maybe, just maybe, this Christmas will be the one that makes my wish come true.

* ❄ *

An hour later, and the cake has been set up, and I'm now adding some finishing touches to the events room, which has been transformed into a winter wonderland.

It snowed overnight, blanketing the parking lot and sidewalks in white. Brooks and Jameson are out front shoveling to ensure the inn's guests and wedding attendees can come and go safely. They're bundled against the cold in thick coats, beanies, and scarves. The latter was a last-minute addition Kay insisted on.

From the window, I watch as Brooks grins at something Jameson says before playfully slugging him on the shoulder. Jameson throws back his head laughing before they go back to shoveling. The brothers' exchange is a simple one, but it tugs at my heartstrings to see them reunited in Starlight Pines, and I know Kay is grateful to have them both here for the holidays.

I check my phone to see that I have a few minutes to spare, so I decide to call Fallon. She's been texting me non-stop, and a quick chat won't hurt before the rest of the vendors and wedding guests start to arrive. I pop in my earbuds so my hands are free while we chat.

"Hey, is everything alright?" Her tone is tinged with worry. "You're usually MIA on wedding days."

"I wanted to wish you a Merry Christmas before things got too hectic. I wish you were here."

"Thanks, Lila. Merry Christmas to you, too." I can hear the

sound of something sizzling on the stove in the background. "What are you making?"

"A caramel glaze for a cinnamon roll wreath," she says in a sing-song voice. "George, the doorman at Harrison's building, doesn't have any family to spend the holidays with, so I thought I'd bring breakfast down to him. Plus, he has three cats of his own, so I'm hoping he has some tips for dealing with this demon cat. The thing acts like he's never seen the inside of an apartment before."

I hate that Fallon is spending her holidays alone in New York. I know she's catering several big events between now and New Year's Day, but she could have flown out here to spend Christmas with me and my family. It's hard to tell if she's truly happy or just puts on a good front. She deserves her own fairy tale ending, although she'd never admit she wants one.

"I'm sure George will appreciate the company," I say, grabbing some silver ribbon to make bows for the back of the chairs. "Unfortunately, I can't help you with your cat problem. Now, if you ever need advice on how to handle a stubborn sausage dog with a mind of his own, I'm your girl."

Fallon bursts out laughing. "Speaking of sausage, anything you want to loop me in on?"

I let out a groan of embarrassment. "Oh. My. God. You did not just say that out loud."

"What?" She feigns innocence. "My best friend is sharing a bed with her brother's hot best friend, and they've already kissed, but I'm not allowed to ask about the juicy details? That's downright cruel."

Sometimes I forget how direct Fallon can be. Her bluntness comes through loud and clear in her texts, but hearing it over the phone takes it to a whole other level.

I glance around the room, making sure I'm alone. "I'm going to tell you something, but you can't freak out, okay?

"Get on with it," she encourages.

"Kay kept Winston at the inn last night, and Brooks and I stayed in my cottage—" I stop mid-sentence when she lets out an excited squeal.

"You totally slept with him, didn't you? Why didn't you say so sooner? Wait, there's more, isn't there?" I have to move the phone away from my ear while she lets out another squeal. "Lila Monroe, you better tell me this instant."

I roll my eyes at her theatrics. "For someone who's sworn off love, you sure sound like a hopeless romantic."

Fallon scoffs. "Don't be ridiculous. I'm just wholly invested in *your* love life. Now tell me, did you sleep with Brooks or not?"

I hadn't planned on telling anyone yet, but she'll keep prying if I don't. And honestly, it's a relief to have someone to confide in. My emotions are all over the map. One part of me is on cloud nine, while the other is bracing to wake up at any second, like Clara in *The Nutcracker*, to find this was all a beautiful illusion.

"It's bad, Fallon. I didn't *just* sleep with Brooks. I'm so into this man I'm pretty sure he ruined me for all other men."

"This is amazing," she shrieks. "I better be your first choice for maid of honor, and I'm still catering your wedding."

I drop the pair of scissors that I was using to cut ribbon.

"Don't you think you're getting ahead of yourself?" I ask, bending down to pick up the scissors. "Brooks and I have only slept in the same bed twice and *slept* together once. That's a far cry from sending out save-the-dates, don't you think?"

I leave out the part where he fucked me several times throughout the night and our little escapade this morning.

"Come on, Lila. This is monumental, and you know it," Fallon says sternly. "Did you guys talk about what you're going to do after the wedding? There's no way he's leaving you after this new development."

It would be nice if I shared her conviction. Honestly, I have no clue what the future holds.

I wish I did.

"We were going to discuss where we go from here, but I had to leave to meet with a vendor," I say, wishing I had the answers both Fallon and I are looking for.

"Well, finish that conversation tonight so you can make things official, and then climb that man like a tree."

"Okay, that's it. I'm cutting off your phone privileges," I chuckle with a small smile. "I've got a wedding to run, so we'll have to chat more about this later."

"You can count on it," she vows.

After she hangs up, I take a moment to survey the room, proud of how the transformation turned out. It's hard to believe Andrew and Hannah's wedding is only hours away, and soon they'll officially be husband and wife.

My excitement falters, the realization sinking in that Brooks could be gone by tomorrow. The thought presses like a weight on my chest, bittersweet and heavy as I try to picture returning to the way things were before him.

The distant sound of voices snaps me out of my melancholy state, and I get back to work adding the last few ribbons to the back of the chairs.

While I can't control much about my current situation, I can ensure every detail of Andrew and Hannah's big day goes off without a hitch.

After that, Brooks and I can figure out what our future holds… or if there's a future for us after all.

CHAPTER 13

Brooks

T HE EVENTS ROOM HAS BEEN TRANSFORMED INTO A winter wonderland, with silver tinsel hanging from the vaulted ceilings and evergreen garlands draped across each beam. Large vases filled with white roses, blue delphiniums, and hypericum berries line the aisle. A frosted blue aisle runner leads to the archway, where the mistletoe I helped Lila hang earlier this week hangs above.

It makes me reflect on how much has shifted this week. When I got here, the idea of enjoying being back in Starlight Pines felt completely foreign. I was a skeptic, set on avoiding my past, and solely focused on my career. Yet, over the past few days, my grandma and Lila have shifted my perspective, truly showing me what I've been missing.

Andrew steps through the door, letting out a low whistle. "Damn, Lila really outdid herself, didn't she?"

I give him a pointed look. "Did you forget I helped?"

He claps me on the back. "Sure, you hung a few decorations, but let's not kid ourselves. She gets all the credit for making Hannah's vision come to life."

"I can't argue with that."

Andrew's wearing a tailored black tux with a silver tie, his hair combed back without a strand out of place.

He got changed in my grandma's office, and Hannah is using the cottage as a bridal suite since Lila insisted that Andrew not see the wedding dress until the ceremony.

"I feel like I should be more nervous," he says, sitting in a nearby chair. "The truth is, I've been waiting for this longer than I care to admit. I knew Hannah was special the day we met, and even though it took us fifteen years, every step along the way was worth it."

I take a seat next to him, leaning back. "How did you know Hannah was the one?"

He told me early on that he liked her, but we've never talked about what made him want to pursue a relationship or ask her to marry him.

"I'll never forget when she gave me an ultimatum," Andrew chuckles. "We had gone to the movies, just the two of us, and were heading to her favorite Italian restaurant. She stopped in the middle of the sidewalk and told me that Mav Miller, a guy she met at the coffee shop she worked at, had asked her out." Andrew's jaw tightens like it's physically painful to think about. "My heart was racing when she admitted she wanted to turn him down but couldn't wait around for me forever. She was frustrated that we spent so much time together, doing all the things couples do, but I never showed interest in taking the next step."

"Why did you wait so long? You never hid the fact that she was off-limits to anyone who came around."

It was the opposite. He threatened every man who even looked at Hannah the wrong way and spent every free minute he had with her. Yet when it came to actually claiming her, it seemed like he couldn't bring himself to cross that line.

He sighs, running a hand through his hair. "You remember what I was like in those early days. I was determined not to let anything stand in the way of my career, and I never saw myself as the type to settle down with a wife and kids. However, the more time I spent with Hannah, the harder it became to imagine my future without her in it." He pauses to adjust his cufflinks. "Her ultimatum was the wake-up call I needed. I couldn't let her walk away and risk losing her to someone else. My only regret is that it took so long to see what was right in front of me."

Andrew and I are alike in how we both put our careers ahead of everything else, but for him, Hannah now takes precedence over everything. I can see why he regrets waiting so long to commit, but in the end, she became the center of his universe, and he wouldn't have it any other way.

Which leaves me wondering where I go from here. If I let what Lila and I have end as nothing more than a fleeting holiday fling, there's a chance I could be stepping away from the best thing to ever happen to me. There's no guarantee that things will work out, but can I really stand the idea of her finding happiness with someone else? Because if I leave, she definitely will. No man would be foolish enough to let someone like her slip away.

So why the hell would I?

This new revelation leaves me with only one choice. I have to come clean to Andrew. If I don't, there's a chance of making everything worse later on.

I clear my throat, my nerves a tight coil in my stomach. "I have something to tell you," I say.

"What is it?" he asks.

"Remember how you asked me if I was interested in Lila?"

He frowns, his face scrunching with concern. "Yeah. What about it?"

Here goes nothing.

"It's complicated, but I do have feelings for her," I admit, bracing for his reaction.

He relaxes back in his chair, folding his arms across his chest.

"Honestly, I can't say I'm surprised. In fact, I'm pretty sure you're the last one to figure it out. Is there a reason you're telling me now?"

"I considered holding off on saying anything until after the wedding, but with you leaving for your honeymoon tonight, I didn't want to risk you hearing it from someone else."

"Is this some holiday fling?" He narrows his eyes. "Because you should know Lila's had a massive crush on you since she was in middle school. Every time I'd visit or call home, she'd ask about you, practically glowing whenever your name came up. And I'm pretty sure she never got over it. So, I'll ask you again, what are your intentions with my sister?" He waits patiently for my answer.

I blow out a deep breath. "What I can say for certain is that she's important to me, and I want her in my life. We haven't had a chance to talk things through yet, but I felt you deserved the truth. You've always been there for me, and I never want to put you in a position where you feel blindsided, especially with Lila involved."

His expression is unreadable as the silence stretches on, and just when I think he's going to get up and walk away, he cracks a faint smile.

"Please explain how you went from coming to Starlight Pines with my sister, the farthest thing from your mind, to now, only four days later, you're telling me you want to be with her?"

"Actually, the first part isn't entirely true," I admit.

Andrew furrows his brow. "What do you mean?"

"At your engagement party, I found Lila hiding out in the photo booth. I ended up joining her, and we talked for a while. It wasn't until later in our conversation that I realized who she was, and I left shortly after. But that hasn't stopped me from thinking about her every day since then."

It's the truth, although I keep the details to myself. The fact that Lila and I kissed in the photo booth is irrelevant to this discussion.

Andrew straightens in his chair, letting out a laugh.

"What's so funny?" I ask.

"It just occurred to me that I unintentionally played match-maker by suggesting you assist her with the wedding."

"My grandma might have something to say about you claiming credit. It's obvious she's been trying to push us together since I got here, although I'm not exactly sure what her angle is. Besides, you might not have anything to worry about. There's a good chance Lila doesn't feel the same way as I do."

He scoffs. "You're joking, right? From the way you two act around each other, it's obvious she never outgrew her feelings for you. If that's true, it means that I'll have to accept that my best friend and my sister are about to officially become an item." He raises a finger, pointing at me. "But let me make one thing clear. If you do anything to hurt her, I won't hesitate to make you regret it. I refuse to stand by if you break her heart. You hear me?"

"I would never hurt her, and you damn well know that," I state. "While I'd like to keep answering your questions, today is about you and Hannah, and according to my watch, we've got less than an hour before the ceremony starts."

Andrew's eyes widen and he jumps out of his chair. "Shit. I still need to finish my vows and throw on my tux jacket."

"Better hurry up. Can't be late to your own wedding," I taunt him.

I'm grateful they've asked me to be a part of their wedding, but selfishly the hardest thing right now is having to wait hours until I get the chance to be alone with Lila again.

Fifty minutes later, Andrew is standing under the archway, and I'm by his side while we wait for the procession to start. Lila is the only bridesmaid, so she'll walk down the aisle before Hannah does.

Andrew adjusts his tie for what must be the hundredth time, his fingers slightly shaking.

I clasp him on the shoulder. "Guess those nerves finally caught up with you,'" I whisper.

"I'm just anxious to have Hannah by my side, is all," he says, smoothing down the lapel of his jacket. "The sooner she's officially my wife, the better."

As if on cue, the opening notes of the processional hum through the air and the small gathering of guests quiet down. I glance at Andrew again, who is watching the doors, impatiently waiting for his bride to walk through them.

I'm more excited for someone else to walk through those doors.

I haven't seen Lila since this morning, and now that I've made up my mind, it feels like each minute is moving at a snail's pace while I wait to talk with her.

When she finally steps inside the room, my jaw drops.

She's wearing a red, form-fitting gown that falls to the floor, and she's holding a small bouquet of white roses in her hand. The tops of her breasts peek out over the delicate sweetheart neckline and the dress accentuates her figure, making it impossible to look away.

Lila glides down the aisle, her lips curved into a dazzling smile that seems to pierce straight through me.

When she reaches the front, she takes her place on the other side of the arch. Her fingers adjust the gold bracelet on her wrist. Her eyes lift to mine, a soft blush coloring her cheeks.

I mouth the words, "You're beautiful."

Her lips form into a tender smile, mouthing back, "Thank you."

Guests rise when Hannah makes her entrance, her off-the-shoulder lace wedding gown shimmers as she moves down the aisle. But my focus remains on Lila for a beat longer, the space between us thick with anticipation.

When Hannah approaches the archway, Andrew is there, extending his hand. He pulls her into his arms, whispering in her ear, and her lets out a laugh.

They step between Lila and me, and once the guests take their seats, Andrew gives a nod to the officiant to begin. The ceremony goes by in a blur, and despite my best efforts to focus on the happy couple, I'm unable to resist stealing glances at Lila, her presence tugging at me like a magnetic force, making it hard to concentrate on anything else.

When it's time for Andrew and Hannah to exchange vows, he takes her hands in his.

"I've spent a lifetime waiting for this day, and nothing makes me happier than knowing you're about to become my wife. I promise to make you laugh during the good times and be your rock through the tough ones. You're my partner, my best friend, and my greatest supporter. When I look back on how far we've come, I know with certainty that we were always meant to find each other, and now that I have you, I promise to cherish you always and forever."

Hannah wipes away a stray tear as she takes a shaky breath.

My eyes dart to Lila, who's holding both her bouquet and Hannah's. She radiates warmth and joy, and I can't seem to look away from her.

"Andrew, from the moment I met you, I knew there was something special between us. It just took you a while to catch up with me." The guests all chuckle. "Today, I stand here, about to become your wife. I will stand by your side through every challenge and celebrate with you through every joy we share. You are my greatest adventure, and I can't wait to spend the rest of my life with you."

My gaze drifts to Lila again, her hand resting over her heart as she watches the couple with admiration.

It strikes me that I want to be *her* greatest adventure. The person she explores the world with and makes new memories alongside. Every other goal I've ever had suddenly pales in comparison to being the person she trusts with her dreams and her heart.

Andrew nudges me with his elbow, a knowing smirk on his face. He holds out his hand, and I pull the ring box from my jacket pocket and hand it over to him. After he and Hannah exchange rings, the officiant pronounces them husband and wife. They share a kiss and then walk back down the aisle hand-in-hand, their faces radiant with joy.

I walk over to Lila and extend my arm. She slides her hand into the crook of my elbow, and we fall in step behind Andrew and Hannah who are greeting guests.

"You're breathtaking," I whisper in her ear. "I couldn't keep my eyes off you."

"And you're quite dashing yourself, Mr. Claus," she grins, shooting me a wink.

Having her by my side is everything I never knew I wanted, let alone needed, and I'm more than ready to make her mine.

CHAPTER 14

Hannah and Andrew's wedding went off without a hitch. I'm usually in the background, observing from a distance, so participating as a bridesmaid this time around was surreal.

For the most part, I was in wedding planner mode, making sure that everything ran smoothly, but I couldn't help stealing glances at Brooks every now and then. He was devastatingly handsome in his tailored suit, the rich charcoal color emphasizing his broad shoulders and strong stance.

I was a goner when he mouthed to me, *"You're beautiful,"* right before Hannah walked down the aisle. It might have been a simple act, but it hit me like a tidal wave. His complement took my breath away and left me smiling like a fool. I've never felt so seen.

After the ceremony, we had dinner and drinks at the inn, followed by a cozy evening by the fireplace, sharing stories and toasting to the happy couple's future.

Andrew surprised Hannah with a honeymoon in Paris, and tonight they're flying out on a private jet, ready to begin their romantic getaway in the city of love.

Not long after they left, Brooks, Winston, and I excused

ourselves, and I didn't miss the silent exchange between Kay and my mom as they watched us head off to my cottage.

When we get inside, Brooks crouches down next to Winston, and my curiosity piques when he pulls a napkin-wrapped bundle from his pocket. Unfolding it, he takes a piece of whatever is inside and offers it to my dog.

"What's that?" I ask.

"Shredded chicken," he replies as Winston eagerly eats it out of his hand. "Funny thing. During dinner, I tried offering him a piece of salmon which he refused, and my grandma informed me that he prefers chicken and peanut butter biscuits."

I shrug, acting oblivious. "And?"

"Interesting how you never said anything about it."

"Had to make you work for his approval, didn't I?"

Winston yips like he's in total agreement. When he's finished, I'm shocked when he nuzzles Brooks' hand—and even more shocked when Brooks scratches behind his ear.

"You're a good boy, aren't you, Winn," he coos.

"I told you he'd grow on you," I tease.

"Only when he's not charging around like a wrecking ball or forcing me to run after him through the snow in bunny slippers."

Once he's finished feeding Winston his treat, he heads to the kitchenette to wash his hands. After drying them, he grabs a box from the counter, one that he must have dropped off earlier.

"What do you have there?" I ask, nodding toward it.

"It's your Christmas present," he says, handing me the box. "I wanted to give it to you earlier, but with the wedding, I didn't have the chance."

"You got me a gift?"

"I did," he confirms with a shrug.

I'm touched by his thoughtfulness and that he went out of his way to pick something out for me, although I can't help but wonder when he had time to get it. I've been so wrapped up in wedding planning that I hadn't considered exchanging gifts, so now I'm left empty-handed.

"That's so sweet, but you didn't have to do that. I feel bad that I didn't get you anything."

He wraps his fingers around mine, brushing a kiss across my knuckles.

"Why don't you check to see what's inside before deciding if a thank you is in order?"

I sit on the edge of the bed, my hands trembling as I unwrap the silver paper and the red bow. As I lift the lid of the box, my breath catches at the sight of a snow globe with a miniature Hollywood Sign, etched with the name of the iconic landmark. I carefully pull it out of the packaging, give it a gentle shake, and watch the snowflakes swirl around the bridge.

"Brooks, it's lovely," I say.

I've wanted a California snow globe to add to my collection since I visited Andrew and Hannah, but it was late in the summer season, and I wasn't able to get one.

"When I found you in that photo booth, I was mesmerized. Even before I knew you weren't a stranger, I was drawn to you. Like earlier today, when everyone else was watching Hannah walk down the aisle, all I could see was you."

It reminds me of my favorite part of weddings when the groom catches his first glimpse of his bride. We might not have been the ones getting married today, but when he looked at me like I belonged to him as we stood across from one another, it felt like a promise of what's to come.

"What are you saying?" My voice is barely above a whisper.

"There's a reason I chose that specific snow globe." He nods to the gift in my hands. "I'm hoping it'll be the start of our adventure," he says, drawing in a deep breath. "I want you to come with me to California." His gaze searches mine for an answer. "You *and* Winston."

"What?" I gasp. I almost drop the snow globe, but Brooks' hand is there to steady me.

"I've cherished every minute with you, and I don't want it to end," he says, gently placing the keepsake on the nightstand and taking my hands in his. "All I'm asking is for the chance to prove that we're meant to be together because I'm not willing to take the chance of losing you."

Is this really happening?

"You mean it? You want us to come stay with you?"

"No, Goldie. I want you and Winston to *live* with me. But if you're not ready for that step yet, I'll take whatever you're willing to give. We could always do half the year in California and the other half in Starlight Pines. I've heard bicoastal couples are all the rages these days," he adds with a teasing smirk.

"What about your company?"

"It would be a challenge, but I'm in this for the long haul, and I'll do anything to make it work. For us."

I tug my bottom lip between my teeth as the wheels turn in my head.

"What about Kay? I can't leave her alone to manage the inn on her own."

"I'm sure she'd be on board with you and Winston coming with me to California."

I playfully swat his chest. "Brooks, I'm serious. Who's going to run the events? Or help her with the day-to-day operations if I'm not here?"

He rubs his thumb against my palm in a soothing stroke. "We'll talk to her at breakfast tomorrow. We can always hire additional staff to lighten her load."

I lean against his chest, inhaling his familiar scent. "What if my quirks bother you? Like my habit of leaving a pile of shoes by the front door. Or the fact that I can't resist playing Christmas music starting in October. And let's not forget the dog hair you'll inevitably find in every corner of your place because I let Winston on the couch and bed."

He places a kiss on my forehead. "We can get a shoe rack if they become a tripping hazard, or I'll just have to perfect my dodging skills," he says, the corner of his mouth lifting into a smile. "Christmas music in October? I'm all for it, as long as the tree goes up early too. And don't worry. I've got a lint roller, and I have an extra pillow Winston can have. So what do you say?"

I tilt my head back, blinking up at him in disbelief.

I've reached a crossroads, the weight of the decision pressing on my chest. The way I see it, there are two options. On one hand, I have the chance to take a leap, leaving behind the comfort of Starlight Pines and venturing into a future that's uncertain but brimming with promise. On the other, I could stay where everything is safe and familiar, but a place I've outgrown.

Suddenly everything becomes clear. After hearing how serious Brooks is about committing, my doubts about this being temporary vanish. The sincerity in his eyes is reassurance that he's all in, making me go weak at the knees. My future is still unclear, but I'm no longer in this alone.

"My answer is yes." I straighten up, making sure he can see the resolve in my eyes.

"To which part?"

"I want to go to California with you, but only if you promise we can come back as often as I want, and if Kay needs help with any upcoming events, I have to be here for those."

"You have my word," he vows. "You can visit whenever you want. All I can hope for is that you and Winston love it so much you'll want to call my place your forever home," he says, his tone resolute.

His response should send me into a panic, worried that we're moving too fast. Instead, it soothes my fears, and I can feel my expression soften.

"Wait. What about Andrew? How do you think he'll handle this?"

I'd never want to jeopardize their friendship, no matter how much I want Brooks.

"I made sure he knew how I felt about you before the wedding."

I blink rapidly, unable to hide my disbelief. "You already talked to him?"

He nods. "I did. He could have reacted negatively, but I wasn't going to wait any longer to make my intentions clear. He did warn me that he'd hurt me if I ever broke your heart." His voice softens as he reaches out to stroke my cheek. "But don't worry, Goldie. I'll spend the rest of my life proving to him and *you* that I'd never do that. You're mine now, and I'll do whatever it takes to keep you that way."

The rest of his life? I'm really his?

"You mean every word, don't you?" I whisper, leaning into his touch.

"I've been yours since the moment you peeked out of that photo booth curtain."

This feels like one of those holiday Hallmark movies I can't get enough of, and part of me is waiting to wake up to discover none of this was real. But the certainty in Brooks' voice and the tenderness of his touch is proof this is my new reality.

He cradles my face in his hands, his lips brushing mine in a tender kiss. "I can't wait to start this adventure with you." He extends his hand. "For tonight though, let me take care of you."

Without hesitation I take his hand, letting him lead me to the bathroom. Once inside he flips on the light before closing the door to give us privacy. Winston will be too busy exploring the new chew toys he got for Christmas to notice we're gone.

Brooks lifts me onto the black marble countertop, leaning in to kiss the tip of my nose.

"What are you doing?" I ask when he goes to the freestanding tub and turns on the faucet.

"You've had a stressful day, so we're going to take a bath." I don't miss the hint of mischief in his tone.

I nod, trusting that whatever he has in store will be worth the wait.

"That's my girl," he says with a satisfied grin. "Stay right there while I fill up the tub."

As the water in the tub rises, he adds a generous pour of a rose petal bubble bath that I had on the ledge, watching as it dissolves into a swirl of pink and white foam. Once the water is high enough, he turns it off, redirecting his focus on me. I beckon him with the crook of my finger.

I let out a shuddered exhale as he advances toward me, his intent unmistakable. This is the start of a new chapter we'll share, and neither of us intends to waste a single second of it.

He positions himself between my legs, firmly gripping my hip with one hand and tilting my chin with the other. His chocolate brown eyes mirror the longing in mine, conveying our deep-seated desire.

"You're perfect." The declaration spills freely from his lips. "Tell me, have you missed my cock today, baby?" He leans in to nibble the shell of my ear.

"Mhmmm," I groan. My panties are wet just thinking about it.

He captures my mouth in a heated kiss, sending a spark of electricity straight to my core. When he takes a step back, I grumble in protest.

"Don't worry. By the time morning comes, I'll have fucked you senseless, and you'll be begging me to stop." He stands up straight, a sly smirk plastered on his face.

I let out a soft hum of approval, thoroughly enjoying the idea.

Brooks is the temptation I'll never be able to resist.

"Let's get you out of that dress," he says. "Stand up, turn around, and put your hands against the counter."

I do as he asks, placing my palms against the cool surface.

Every cell in my body is on fire as he pushes my hair over my shoulder, leaving my back exposed. He places one hand firmly on my hip and uses the other to slowly drag down the zipper of my dress. The suspense is unbearable. I exhale sharply as he grinds his rigid cock against my ass.

"You like that?" he whispers in my ear. "Thinking about my cock inside that tight cunt of yours?"

"Oh god, yes," I mewl.

He brushes my dress off my shoulders, and I feel his breath against my skin seconds before he presses kisses down my neck. He unclasps my bra, releasing my aching breasts from their confines, and reaches around to brush my nipples with the tips of his fingers in teasing strokes. I whimper when he rolls my nipples between his fingers, pinching them roughly.

"I love that you're always so responsive," Brooks states.

"Only for you," I murmur.

"That's right—just for me."

I whine in protest when he releases my nipples.

He pulls my dress down the rest of the way, letting it pool at my feet, before spinning me around to face him. He traces his fingers down my leg until he gets to my panties, dragging them down my legs.

"I'm keeping these," he states, setting them on the counter beside me. "Hold on tight, beautiful," he urges.

I secure my hands on his shoulders, and he scoops me into his arms, setting me back down on the counter. He's keeping me in a state of suspense, teetering on the brink of anticipation. I'll lose my mind if he doesn't give me more—and fast.

"Brooks, I *need* you, please."

"Good things come to those who wait remember?" he says with a teasing grin as he brushes a strand of hair behind my ear.

My mouth goes dry when he pulls his shirt over his head, revealing his rock-solid chest. His breath hitches when I lean forward, tracing every definition of his abs with my fingers. As I trail my finger toward his V-line, he moves back, stripping out of the rest of his clothes.

"Brooks?" I moan in frustration.

"Patience, beautiful."

He works his hand up and down his thick shaft. I'm mesmerized as he strokes, starting at the bottom and reaching the tip, smearing the drop of pre-cum over the crown of his dick.

"Watch what you fucking do to me, Lila." He glances down at his erect cock as he moves his hand up and down his shaft. His eyes are sinfully dark, his jaw tense, his nostrils flaring. He looks wild, uninhibited, and all mine.

His dark brown eyes sear into me like he's marking me in more ways than one, only leaving my face long enough to look down to where his cock is aimed. He groans as he angles himself at my entrance, ropes of cum spurting onto my bare skin as he finds his release. One hand coaxes every last drop from the head of his cock, the other smearing it along my exposed thighs and pussy.

He's the director, and I'm the script he's bringing to life.

A tale of longing, desire, and a love story that's only beginning to unfold.

"You're mine, beautiful," he murmurs before he crashes his mouth to mine, giving me a passionate kiss.

His cock is still hard as he draws his cum on my skin with the tip before pushing inside me in a single, deep thrust, his patience long gone.

Oh. My. God.

"I'll never get enough of this pussy of yours," he says in a guttural tone.

I wind my hands around his neck, tangling my fingers in his hair as he pushes in and out in deep, steady thrusts, savoring the moment. I moan in delight, relishing the fact that I'm stuffed full of his length.

He grips my chin with his hand while he relentlessly pounds into me. "You're everything I've ever wanted. Promise we're in this together."

"Always." I caress his cheek.

His eyes blaze with lust as he watches me roll my clit between my fingers, pinching it when I'm on the verge of falling apart. Soon we're both barreling toward our release.

"Brooks, I'm going to…"

I throw my head back as my orgasm crashes over me, riding the euphoric wave for as long as I can. Brooks holds me close as we both come down from our heightened state.

He presses a kiss to my forehead. "Still want a bath?" he asks before he slowly pulls out of me.

I nod, wanting to savor the quiet calm a little while longer.

Once he's refilled the bathtub, he helps me into the piping hot water and settles behind me. I welcome the accompanying sting, letting the heat soak through my tense muscles. The smell of roses envelops the room with a sense of tranquility.

I lean back against Brooks' chest as he wraps his arms around me.

Every muscle in my body relaxes as his lips graze my shoulder. He plants featherlight kisses against each freckle. "This is the first year I've felt the holiday spirit since losing my dad, and it's all thanks to you," he murmurs.

I tip my head back to look at him. "Why do you say that?"

"Because this year, Christmas brought me you."

CHAPTER 15

T HE NEXT MORNING WE'RE HAVING BREAKFAST AT THE dining room table with Kay and Jameson. Now that the wedding is over, things at the inn have calmed down so Lila has some down time.

She nibbles on her lower lip as she wrings her hands. "Kay, I have something I'd like to talk to you about."

We agreed it would be easier to share the news about Lila coming with me to California and us becoming a couple in one go—two birds, one stone.

While Lila has been beside herself with worry, I'm optimistic that we'll be able to come up with a solution to ensure that Grandma isn't left to manage the inn on her own. I haven't had a chance to discuss things with Jameson, but I'm glad he's here.

"Is this about you leaving?" Grandma asks Lila point-blank.

Lila crinkles her brow. "Um… Yes, but how did you know that?"

She glances over at me, and I hold out my hands in defense. "I haven't said anything."

Grandma waves us off with a laugh. "Oh, sweetheart, no one needed to tell me. I'm not new to this. You've been restless since you went to Andrew and Hannah's engagement party, and I didn't miss how whenever Brooks' name was mentioned, your face lit up like a Christmas tree. Once I saw that he was just as smitten, it was clear where things were headed. You both simply needed a slight nudge in the right direction, is all."

Wait a minute.

"Hey, Grandma. You never explained why you never offered me one of those fold-out beds when you found out my cot broke."

She shrugs. "There was a lot going on and it slipped my mind."

I'm still not convinced, which leads me to suspect Grandma has been busy pulling the strings behind the scenes, trying to get Lila and me together. It was a gamble, but she has an uncanny ability to stack the odds in her favor, leaving me to wonder if it's luck or pure genius.

She reaches over to pat me on the cheek. "You're thinking too hard, dear," she says before turning her attention back to Lila. "You have nothing to worry about. I won't be on my own when you leave. Jameson told me earlier that he'll be spending a lot more time in Starlight Pines. Dr. Dancliff, who owns a pediatric practice in town, is cutting back his hours, and Jameson is going to help him out two days a week."

My brother avoids my gaze while pouring himself a glass of orange juice. Now that I think about it, he's been strangely quiet since he got here. He's the Chief of Pediatrics at a world-renowned hospital, is on the advisory board for the World Health Organization's pediatric care division, and is credited for founding a free clinic program for underserved kids in New York City. So I have no idea how he'll find the time to travel back and forth each week, but something tells me he has his reasons.

I make a mental note to ask him about it later.

"Who's going to help out when Jameson's busy with work or in New York?" Lila asks Grandma. "You can't manage the event planning on your own." Her voice slightly trembles.

This is not going how I thought it would, and at this rate, I'm afraid Lila might reconsider her decision. She has a heart of gold, and until she's sure my grandma has all the support she needs at the inn, she won't want to leave.

Grandma's face lights up with a smile. "Don't worry. I've already sorted that out."

Lila looks surprised. "You have?"

"Yes, a woman reached out about a job, and I hired her. Her name is Sutton. She and her daughter, Penny, were passing through on Christmas Eve and stopped to see Santa—or should I say you," Grandma says to me with a wink. "They're looking for a place to call home, and they fell in love with Starlight Pines. Sutton noticed we were short-staffed and called to ask if we had any openings. I hired her on the spot. Originally, I had planned for her to take over housekeeping and was going to put her and Penny in a room on the first floor. But now that the cottage is open, they can stay there. It'll give them a roof over their head and some extra space while Sutton gets back on her feet.

Jameson, who's been a silent observer until now, spits out the orange juice he was sipping. "Grandma, you can't offer a random woman a job because you feel sorry for her. Let alone offer her a place to stay."

Grandma sits up straight, squaring her shoulders. "Why the hell not? This is my inn, is it not? Which means I decide who stays here and who doesn't, thank you very much."

It's on the tip of my tongue to point out that she used the same language she reprimanded me for, but hold back when she raises an eyebrow, daring me to challenge her.

"I don't want her trying to take advantage of you," Jameson says, his voice softening.

"Nonsense. In case you forgot, I've been doing this long before you were born," she retorts. "And besides, it'll be nice to have a child around to bring some life to the place. I'll need someone to spoil now that Winson's off to California with Lila."

"We won't be gone forever. Think of it as an extended vacation," Lila says, but her tone betrays her. "And we'll visit as often as we can."

"Mmm, we'll see about that, won't we?" Grandma says with a raised brow.

Yes, we will.

Like I told Lila earlier, if things go according to plan, she and Winston will love California so much they'll want to make it their new home and stay with me forever.

After brunch, Lila and I take Winston on a walk into town. Today, he's decked out in a new candy cane striped sweater that Lila's mom gave him for Christmas. He also got a giant bag of peanut butter biscuits and a new stuffed hippo since his current one is missing an ear.

I never imagined that my world would revolve around a bossy dachshund and his sunshine owner. Yet now that I've had a glimpse of what life is like with Lila and Winston, I realize just how empty mine was until they came along.

A few locals are milling around town, taking in the fresh air after celebrating Christmas at home. We stopped by Sip & Savor, the local coffee shop, to grab drinks to go.

"Here we are," I say as I step outside with our order.

"Thanks." Lila beams when I hand her a toasted white chocolate mocha. "Why do all the best flavors have to be seasonal?"

"Don't worry, California has plenty of coffee shops with creative baristas. I'm sure they'd be happy to make you a toasted white chocolate mocha in the middle of June if that's what you want."

"And what if Winston and I don't stay that long?"

"Then I guess you'll be resigned to a life without seasonal coffee flavors year-round," I say, crossing my arms with a teasing grin. "Although I have a feeling you'll like it there."

"Oh yeah? And why is that?" Lila asks.

"Because staying with me comes with daily foot massages, morning coffee, and binge-watching all your favorite shows together."

"How romantic."

"Did I mention orgasms? Lots and lots of orgasms."

She covers her face as she bursts out laughing. "Promises, promises."

"Ones I have every intention of making good on," I say, leaning over to give her a quick peck on the lips. "Now all that's left is making sure Winston has a mountain of toys and an endless treat supply to keep him entertained at night while we're… busy."

Lila places her hands on her hips, glancing down at the dog in question. "What do you think, Winston? Think you can handle being bribed to sleep in your dog bed every now and then?"

He barks in agreement, and when I look down, he's on his hind legs, pawing at the air. His eyes are locked on the pup cup in my hand as if it's a prize he's about to claim.

"Relax, buddy, it's all yours."

When I bend down and offer it to him, he nearly knocks me over as he dives in, devouring his treat with gusto.

Lila laughs at his enthusiasm, shaking her head. "Did I mention whipped cream is another one of his favorite treats?"

"Duly noted," I say, storing that information for later.

Once Winston is finished, I toss the empty cup, pull out a red envelope from my coat pocket and hand it to Lila.

"What's this?" she asks. "You already got me a present."

"This belongs to you, and I figured now was as good a time as any to return it."

Lila's mouth falls open when she pulls out the black-and-white Polaroid strip of us from Andrew and Hannah's engagement party.

Her fingers trace the photos, her mouth curving into a smile. "Brooks, this is incredible."

"I'm glad you like it."

I convinced my assistant, in exchange for an added bonus, to stop by my house on Christmas Eve and retrieve the photo strip I had tucked away in my nightstand for safekeeping. He was able to expedite shipping so it arrived in Starlight Pines this morning. It was well worth it to see the smile on Lila's face.

"I can't believe you took these," she says. "They were gone when I checked, so I assumed they never printed."

"I wasn't ready to let that memory go, and I wanted something tangible to hold on to."

"I'm so happy you did." She wraps her arm around me. "I can't wait to frame it, although it's going to be tough deciding on which kind to get. Does gold or silver match the décor in your apartment, or what about something bold like a colorful statement piece?"

"Pick whichever frame you like, as long as you promise it'll go in the living room so everyone who comes to visit knows how much you mean to me," I state.

"You've got yourself a deal."

We make our way to a bench near the coffee shop facing the park with the town Christmas tree. I hoist Winston up beside Lila. Once we're seated, I casually drape my arm around her shoulders. There's no one else I'd rather spend the holidays with, or any day for that matter. I'm still in disbelief that she's really mine. *Completely, irrevocably mine.*

I lean over, cupping her jaw in my hand, and kiss her deeply. The noise around us dims, replaced by the quiet certainty that this is exactly where I'm meant to be.

"I'm really glad you came back to Starlight Pines," Lila murmurs.

"Me too."

For the longest time, I viewed life through a haze of skepticism and disappointment. I avoided the town my dad adored, too afraid to believe that happiness was possible here, convinced it would lead to more heartache. As snowflakes drift around me, I can't help but think that he played a part in bringing me back here and that he would want me to make new memories that honor Grandma and the place he cherished most.

Then, Lila stepped into my life—or rather, I stepped *back* into hers. She showed me how to appreciate the small things and reminded me that happiness can often be found where you least expect it, even in a small town I thought I had left behind for good.

After all these years, I finally feel like I'm home. It's not the place that matters but the person who makes even the smallest moments extraordinary—and for me, that's Lila. What we experienced wasn't just holiday spirt, it was the start of a new beginning. By opening my heart again, I found a magic that will last forever.

EPILOGUE

Brooks

TWO MONTHS LATER

AS SOON AS I PUSH OPEN THE DOOR TO MY APARTMENT, Winston darts down the hallway, yipping with excitement. Today, he's sporting a blue-and-white snowflake sweater that Lila's mom mailed last week. The fact that he no longer lives in Starlight Pines hasn't stopped her from spoiling him one bit.

I bend to give him a good scratch behind the ear. He sniffs at me, nudging his warm nose against my coat pocket.

"Caught me red-handed, didn't you?"

His ears perk up the second I take out the peanut butter biscuit. When I hold it out for him, his tail starts wagging furiously, and he wastes no time gobbling it up.

"Winston, what are you—" I rise to my feet as Lila rounds the corner. "Brooks, you're home," she exclaims, throwing her arms around me.

I lift her into my arms, and she squeals with delight, her contagious smile lighting up the room as I hold her close. I still can't believe how lucky I am to have her in my life.

When I set her down, I notice her hair is pulled into a messy bun, and she has blue and pink glitter dusting her cheeks, as if she's stepped out of a whimsical daydream.

"Working on some kind of art project?" I tease, brushing a stray fleck of glitter from the bridge of her nose.

"The bride wants to include glitter wine glasses in her bridal shower gift boxes. I decided to make them myself, but now my office looks like a glitter factory explosion. I'd suggest steering clear unless you want to end up sparkling for the next month. Although I do think you'd wear it well," she laughs, pretending to flick glitter onto me. "How was work today?"

"I missed you," I say, earning a sharp bark from Winston. "Yes, I missed you too, Winn." His tail wags triumphantly as if my response meets his approval.

"We're glad you're home," Lila says, lifting up on her toes to kiss me.

I can't help but grin every time she calls our apartment home.

We stayed in Starlight Pines until after New Year's. She packed up the cottage, bringing most of her things to California while the rest went into her parents' attic—for now.

We're already been back twice since then, and we've got a trip planned to France with Lila's family this summer. I'm not wasting any time giving her the chance to begin exploring the world.

Before we left Starlight Pines during the holidays, I spoke with my grandma and learned that no one had carried on my dad's legacy of making sure every child had gifts under the tree at Christmas, and I knew it was time to bring the Holiday Claus Foundation back to life. But instead of limiting it to Starlight Pines, the goal is to grow the foundation into a nationwide effort. Lila and Jameson have offered to help, by this coming holiday season, we'll be helping families across the country create unforgettable Christmas memories.

Soon after Lila and I arrived in California, I had to return to work. Not one to sit idle, Lila spent her first few weeks in town, helping Hannah out at her yoga studio. Winston tagged along, and they spent the afternoons exploring the city. While it kept them busy, I could tell Lila missed the energy and creativity of organizing events.

I planned on helping her set up her own agency when she was ready, but then fate intervened. She overheard a woman at the yoga studio mention that their wedding planner had quit. Lila offered her services, and fast forward six weeks, and she's now booked solid through September. Our spare bedroom has been transformed into her workspace.

Now, instead of finding excuses to stay at the office, I'm out the door by five. We spend our nights taking Winston on walks to the nearby dog park, where he enjoys terrorizing the squirrels, chasing them up the trees while Lila and I stroll hand in hand, laughing at his antics.

My nights are spent worshiping every inch of Lila's body and showering her with affection. I'm addicted to the way her body fits perfectly against mine, and savor every soft gasp and moan that passes her mouth.

"Lila," I murmur.

She gazes up at me with those bright blue eyes I could get lost in for hours. "Yeah?"

"Move in with me," I state.

She tilts her head, her brow knitting together. "We're living together now, aren't we?" She motions around the apartment.

She's right. Her throw pillows are scattered across the couch, the Polaroids from the photo booth are framed on the coffee table, and her snow globes are arranged on a display shelf in the corner. I can't wait to add to her collection, marking the places we'll explore together. The world is hers to discover, and I'll be right there with her for every new adventure.

"Yes, but I want to make it official. During our next visit to Starlight Pines, let's get the rest of your things from your parents' house and bring them here. This is your home, and it's where I want us to build our future."

We told her parents we were together the day after breaking the news to my grandma. Her mom wasn't the least bit surprised, and though her dad initially had reservations, mainly because of our age difference, he's warming up to the idea after seeing how much Lila means to me.

She's become my everything, and there's nothing I wouldn't do for her. I've held back my true feelings, worried it was too soon, yet this moment seems like the perfect one to speak my truth.

I gently lift her chin, meeting her mesmerizing blue-green gaze. "I love you, Lila Monroe. I love you so damn much."

She places her hand over mine, her voice a whisper. "I love you too, Brooks Claus."

Later that night, Lila and I are curled up on the couch watching *The Holiday.* It's one of the few holiday movies I haven't seen, and though it's almost March, I don't mind watching it, considering Lila's in my arms, and the warmth of her presence makes it feel like Christmas never ended.

I pause the movie when Lila's phone rings. There's only one person who would be calling at this time, and the conversation could last for hours, depending on the latest drama Fallon has to share. I haven't met her yet, but Lila's planning a trip for us to visit New York next month.

If there's one thing I've learned listening to their conversations it's that Harrison Stafford is enemy number one. And he has a demon cat that takes pleasure in tormenting Fallon.

Thank God, Winston and I get along for the most part. There's no question who Lila would put in the dog house if she had to choose between us.

"Hi, Fallon," Lila answers. "You're on speaker."

"I'm so glad you picked up," Fallon says, her voice frantic. "I may have done something really stupid, and I have no clue how to fix it."

"Woah, slow down," Lila says. "What happened?"

"Remember that prank I told you about last week?"

Lila's eyes widen, and she covers her hand over her mouth. "Please tell me you didn't actually go through with that."

I wonder which prank she's referring to. Since Harrison came home from visiting his family for the holidays and found his hockey stick bedazzled, it's been one prank after another—each one more elaborate than the last.

"It was an accident… sort of," Fallon rushes to explain. "I bought the bleach and put it in Harrison's shampoo bottle, but after I talked with you, I decided not to go through with it. Then the timer went off for the quiche I had in the oven, and I had a client call after that, and it slipped my mind."

"I understand, but that's a pretty big thing to forget about, don't you think?" Lila asks gently.

Fallon groans. "Yeah, I know. I didn't even think about it again until I heard Harrison shouting in his bathroom. When I ran in to check on him… well, that's not important. All that matters is that his hair is bright orange, and if I don't fix this, he'll probably kick me out."

"Can you blame him?" Lila says bluntly.

"Not helpful," Fallon mutters.

Lila blows out a breath. "You're right. What about a color-correcting shampoo? It should help balance out the brass-iness in his hair. It could take a few days though."

"I don't have a *few* days. He has an important business meeting tomorrow morning that he can't miss, and he absolutely cannot show up with orange hair," Fallon says, her voice tight with frustration.

Lila chews on her lower lip as she thinks. She glances over when I give her leg a light squeeze and mute the call.

"What is it?" she asks.

"He's the CEO of a multi-billion-dollar company, right? Have his assistant pull some strings and get a colorist over to his apartment tonight. I bet someone will do it for the right price."

She laughs. "Naturally, your suggestion is to throw money at the problem… although I have to admit, in this situation, it's a genius idea."

"I've been known to have those on occasion," I say with a smirk.

I'm glad I'm not on the receiving end of one of Fallon's pranks and that Lila isn't interested in pulling those kinds of stunts.

"Lila, are you there?" Fallon asks, her voice panicked.

She quickly kisses me before unmuting the call. "I'm here. Have Harrison reach out to his assistant and explain the situation. They'll be able to find someone who can come to his penthouse tonight to fix it."

"That's a great idea," Fallon exclaims. "I better go. Harrison is getting more anxious by the second and won't stop running his hands through his hair like that'll fix it."

"Of course, that's what friends are for. Keep me updated," Lila says.

"Will do. Bye," Fallon says before ending the call.

Lila sets her phone down on the cushion and climbs into my lap, resting her head against my chest.

"Sounds like there's trouble in paradise," I tease.

"Fallon claims she's only working for Harrison, but it's obvious there's more to it than they're willing to admit. I only hope they figure it out before their pranks cause real trouble."

"I'm sure they'll manage." I tilt her chin so her eyes meet mine. "I love you, Lila."

Since saying those three little words out loud, I can't help but feel an undeniable sense of relief and a desire to remind her how much she means to me as often as possible.

"I love you too, Brooks. Always."

I never imagined I'd be lucky enough to find true happiness, but here I am, holding the woman of my dreams in my arms, proving that love is real and worth waiting for.

Want to find out what happens next Christmas Eve when Brooks pops a life-changing question? Plus, get an exclusive sneak peek of Jameson and Sutton's swoon-worthy holiday romance. Type this link into your browser to read the extended epilogue for *The Holiday Claus:*
https://BookHip.com/XXVDAXL

Thank you for taking the time to read *The Holiday Claus.* If you enjoyed this book, please consider leaving a review on your preferred platform(s) of choice. It's the best compliment I can receive as an author, and it makes it easier for other readers to find my books.

OTHER BOOKS BY ANN EINERSON

If You Give a Grump a Holiday Wishlist (Presley & Jack)
A small town, fake dating, one bed spicy workplace holiday romance.

If You Give a Single Dad a Nanny (Dylan & Marlow)
A swoon worthy, single dad/nanny, age gap, he's grumpy, she's sunshine, banter-filled spicy small town romance

If You Give a Billionaire a Bride (Cash & Everly)
A marriage of convenience that starts with a Vegas wedding between a reformed playboy and his best friend's sister in a banter-filled spicy billionaire romance

When You Give a Lawyer (Dawson & Reese)*a Kiss is a standalone workplace romance between a grumpy billionaire and his new assistant in an age gap, banter-filled, spicy love story.*

The Spotlight (Conway & Sienna)*A best friend's brother, opposites attract, dating in secret, spicy rockstar romance.*

ACKNOWLEDGMENTS

There are so many people who made this book possible, and I can't thank you all enough for your love, kindness, and support. The Holiday Claus wouldn't have been possible without each and every one of you.

To Bryanna—For being the best co-worker and collaborator. You make the day-to-day of being a writer so much more fun and far less lonely, and am grateful for your friendship always.

To Autumn—I'm so lucky our paths crossed. Thanks for your blunt honesty when I need to hear it and your dedication to helping me achieve my goals. I couldn't do this without you.

To Kait, Tab and Kaity—Words cannot adequately express my gratitude for you. Thank you for putting up with my endless DMs, questions, and concerns. Your feedback is invaluable and this story would never have made it down on paper without you cheering me on from the sidelines.

To Jess and Kenz—Thank you for helping to spread the word about The Holiday Claus and for your creative input. Your ability to bring my vision to life always amazes me and I'm so incredibly grateful to work alongside each of you.

To Jeannine, Lyndsey, Rebecca, Tina, and Courtney—I couldn't have asked for a better editing team. I'm grateful for your expertise and for pushing me to write a story worth reading.

To Caroline, Wren, Lauren Brooke, Jessa Lynn, Hunter, Kat, and Sammie, Ada—Your honest, detailed, and candid feedback drove me to create the best possible version of this book. Thank you!

To Madison—For designing the most adorable cover for this book. It was love at first sight and it makes my heart so happy that my readers love it just as much as I do.

To Sandea, Roxan, and Randy—You taught me to believe in myself and to chase my dreams, no matter the cost. I love you always.

To Kyler—Thank you for supporting my insane work schedule while in the midst of moving across the world. Without you my dream of becoming a full-time author wouldn't have come true.

To my ARC team—Even before you saw the cover, read the book, or fell in love with Brooks & Lila's love story, you gave The Holiday Claus a chance. Thank you for all your thoughtful messages, posts, stories, reviews, and comments. Your endless love and support never ceases to amaze me.

Most importantly, thank **YOU**. There are so many incredible books to choose from and I'm honored you took a chance on my story. None of this would be possible without you! Every single tag, share and DM means the world and motivates me to keep writing on the days I think this might be for nothing. I hope you enjoyed your time in Starlight Pines with Brooks, Lila and Winston.

ABOUT THE AUTHOR

Ann Einerson is the author of imperfect contemporary love stories that will keep you invested until the very last page.

Ann writes dirty-mouthed heroes who love to spoil their women, often fall first, and enjoy going toe-to-toe with their fierce heroines. Each of Ann's books features a found family, an ode to her love of travel, and serves plenty of banter and spice. Her novels are inspired by the ample supply of sticky notes she always has on hand to jot down the stories that live rent-free in her mind.

When she's not writing, Ann enjoys spoiling her chatty pet chickens, listening to her dysfunctional playlists, and going for late-night treadmill runs. She lives in Michigan with her husband.

KEEP IN TOUCH WITH ANN EINERSON

Website:

www.anneinerson.com

Newsletter:

www.anneinerson.com/newsletter-signup

Instagram:

www.instagram.com/authoranneinerson

TikTok:

www.tiktok.com/@anneinersonbooks

Amazon:

www.amazon.com/author/anneinerson

Goodreads:

www.goodreads.com/author/show/29752171.Ann_Einerson

www.ingramcontent.com/pod-product-compliance
Lightning Source LLC
Chambersburg PA
CBHW031601310726
48974CB00003B/760